THE LADY OF ROLIKA

Books by Brendan Noble

The Frostmarked Chronicles:
A Dagger in the Winds
The Trials of Ascension
The Daughters of the Earth
The Deathless Sons

Frostmarked Tales:
The Rider in the Night
The Lady of Rolika

The Prism Files:
The Fractured Prism
Crimson Reigns
Pridefall
White Crown

Author Note: Trigger Warning

The Lady of Rolika contains elements that may be triggers or traumatic to some readers, so please proceed with caution if any of the below are so for you. I have done my best to treat these serious topics carefully and with respect.

- Suicide
- Self-harm
- Sexual Assault

Major Gods and Their Marks

Marzanna - Frostmark
Winter, Disease, and Death

Dziewanna - Bowmark
Wilds, Hunt, and Spring

Jaryło - Springmark
Spring, Agriculture, and War

Mokosz - Mothermark
Women and Divination

Perun - Thundermark
Thunder, Justice, and War

Weles - Serpentmark
Underworld and Lowlands

Swaróg - Forgemark
Celestial Fire and Smithing

Dadźbóg - Sunmark
The Sun

Pronunciation Guide

Major Characters

Kostroma: Kohstrohmah
Minna: Meenah
Kupalo: Koopahloh

Gods

Marzanna: Mahrzahnah
Simargł: Seemahrgwuu
Perun: Pehruun
Strzybóg: Strihbohg
Weles: Vehlehs
Jaryło: Yahrihwoh
Dadźbóg: Dahdzbohg
Czarnobóg: Charhnohbohg

Other Terms

Rolika: Rohleekah
Solga(wie): Sohlgah(vee)
Žityje: Zhihtyeh
Szeptucha: Shehptuuhah
Krowik(ie): Krohvihk(ee)
Miawka: Meeahvkah
Upiór: Uupeeohr
Jawia: Yahveeah
Prawia: Prahveeah
Nawia: Nahveeah

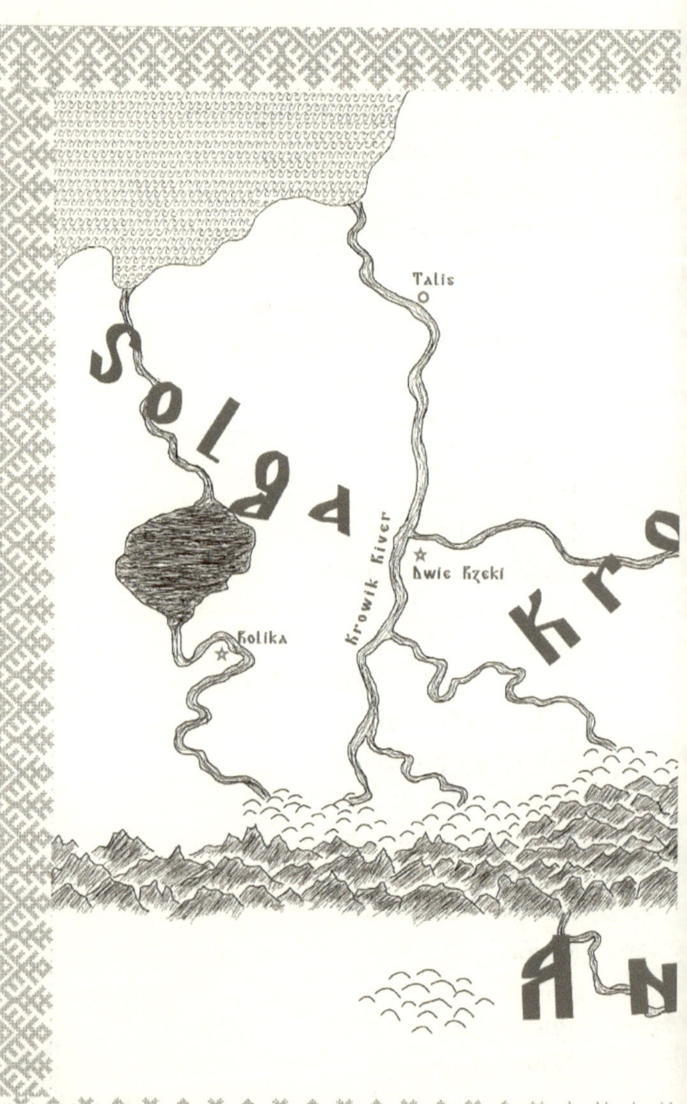

Solga
Talis
Krowik River
Dwie Rzeki
Kolika
Kro
An

WIK
Klist
Mangled Woods
Frostmarked Horde
Bustelintin
Harrow Pass
Wyzra River
Kynnytsia
Małe Wzgòrze
Astiw
Behmir River
Southern Hills
Huebia
Vastroth
Vora
Tior River
Skeresy
Telem

A FROSTMARKED TALE

THE LADY OF ROLIKA

BRENDAN NOBLE

1

Minna

"The lands shall fall." *Clang.*

"The rivers shall freeze." *Clang.*

"Walls will crumble before her might." *Clang.*

"The lands shall fall." *Clang.*

"The rivers shall freeze." *Clang.*

"Walls will—"

"Oi!" One of the ill-fated guards barked from the other side of the bars. Pig-headed idiot that one, always sticking his finger up his nose and other places it didn't belong... "Shut it or I'll rip out that tongue of yours!"

The other shook his head. Bald and stocky, patches of discolored skin covered his exposed scalp. Like a mutt that'd been shaved for disobedience. Minna smirked at that thought. "Witch just keeps saying that same chant over and over," he grumbled. "Not worth yelling. Just 'bout got it memorized by this point."

Sending her iron shackles into the bars once again, Minna clicked her tongue and studied them with her one good eye. *Chant?* No, this was no chant. Nor was she a witch.

These were the words Lady Marzanna had tasked Minna, her *most* loyal szeptucha, with sharing among all the people of Jawia. To bring the news of the winter goddess's reign. First in Vastroth, and now in Solga.

"The oppressed and ruined shall rise as one," she hissed, striking the bars once more. "Your queen and false gods shall collapse at Lady Marzanna's feet. For only she will reign and—"

"All others will weep in blood," Mutt finished with a dismissive wave. "Yeah, yeah, we know…"

"Yet you are too stupid to comprehend!" Minna shouted before slamming the shackles again. Why were they all too stupid?

Pig wagged his scratching finger and approached her cell. His steps echoed through the stone walls. Good. That meant her words did so as well. Lady Marzanna would never have let Minna languish where her message went unheard. Why would the goddess abandon her most faithful szeptucha?

"What a pretty young thing like you do to get locked up her?" Pig asked, his deep blue eyes boring into hers.

Mutt scoffed. "Not shutting up apparently. Just look at that scarred eye of hers. That worm's crawled where she shouldn't have I reckon."

Pig cocked his eyed, clutching his short spear as he stood at the bars. "You bed the wrong man?"

Jaryło's loins, they're as dumb as they look. And they sure looked dumb in those undersized blue tunics, covered in chain mail that only stretched to the middle of their forearms. When they raised their arms, Minna could see their wide stomachs. These people had no clue how easily they would fall to Lady Marzanna if even their guards were so flabby.

"Nah." Mutt sniffled and ran his snot across his short sleeve. "She musta insulted The Lady."

Minna's hand shot through the bars, entrapping Pig's throat. "There is only one lady! One goddess! All others are false!"

Mutt scrambled for his spear that rested against the wall as his comrade sputtered. They believed Minna to be just a weak girl. Oh, how little they knew. *I should kill them both…*

"No!" a voice hissed in her head. Lady Marzanna's voice. *"They shall witness the miracle of your escape. Now is the day. I am ready."*

Listening to her goddess, Minna released Pig as Mutt rushed the cage. By the time he stabbed at her, she was already out of reach. *Idiots.* But Lady Marzanna had given them a purpose. All living beings had been given a purpose by her. Even pigs and mutts.

With a flip of her braided brown hair, Minna bowed to the guards. "You should be honored. Lady Marzanna has chosen you for a very important purpose."

The guards exchanged glances. "Nonsense again," Mutt said with a shrug.

Frost met Minna's fingers as she knelt and placed her palm to the stone floor. Cold. These Solgawi didn't bother to offer their prisoners any heat. For most, they probably just hoped the underfed criminals would freeze to death. Minna was no underfed criminal.

Drawing in the chill, the Frostmark upon her scarred eye seared as she whispered in the old tongue, "*Pri.*" Push.

Žityje—the life force fueling a szeptucha's channeling—rushed from her as a sheet of ice slammed into the bars.

The guards scrambled out of the way just before the bars spun down the stone hall. Without even a glance at their spears, they quivered on the ground as Minna stepped free from her cell and sneered down at them. "Go. Tell your people that Lady Marzanna has come, that they will die if they do not surrender their worship of the false goddess you call The Lady."

"Who… Who are you?" Pig stuttered.

Lady Marzanna cackled in Minna's mind as she ran her finger along a shard of ice embedded in the stone wall. "I am the messenger, the first. My name matters not, only the words I bring. You know them, so if you want to live, I suggest you spread them with the fury of a blizzard."

She didn't wait to hear their reply.

"You did well, my little one," Lady Marzanna said as Minna strode down the hall, the skirts of her deep blue dress sweeping behind her with each silent step. *"Now free yourself and find The Lady. The Solgawi await…"*

"Yes, my goddess."

Other prisoners shouted from behind their bars as she passed, screaming for her to let them out. But they were foolish men. Rapists. Murders. Lady Marzanna did not protect those who abused their strength. She punished them.

Fist clenched, Minna grasped her goddess's power. Anger swelled within it. Against the Betrayer, Jaryło. Against the scum behind those bars. And against all who dared to oppose her.

Screams replaced the shouts. Then silence.

Before her, Minna's breaths turned to fog as a welcomed chill met her skin. It had amazed her once how quickly Lady Marzanna's power could freeze a room, but in time, the cold had become a loving companion. The same could not be said for the prisoners. Minna grinned as she marched past their corpses, some of them still frozen with arms outstretched toward her. If she'd had more time, she would've granted these soon-to-be demons Lady Marzanna's Frostmark. But she had more important things to do.

Footsteps approached from around the corner. Slow. These guards were used to prisoners screaming for freedom, and few were sober, let alone attentive.

Minna took a frosted breath, summoning a dagger of ice as the pair of guards reached the corner. The first muttered under his breath before glancing at his partner. "Should've brought my—"

The dagger pierced his throat with ease and turned his words into incoherent gurgling. Not that the guards ever said anything worth hearing anyway. Before the second guard could attack, Minna spun and sent a blast of ice into the base of his spear and then into his hand, effectively pinning him in place.

"Who are you?" he spat.

Why do they all ask that?

"I am the messenger, the first…" she repeated for the thousandth time. "Be glad Lady Marzanna wishes for most of you to live."

With that, she swept down the final hall and out of the dungeon. Two more guards awaited her outside, but they seemed shocked to see a bruised, disheveled woman walking through the doors. That made freezing their boots to the ground simple. Though they shouted for reinforcements, Minna decided it best not to freeze their tongues. Lady Marzanna would want them able to speak.

The city beyond was unlike any of the scattered villages of Krowik or the stacked limestone buildings of Vastroth. Pillars of smoke rose from wood and gray stone buildings constructed on stilts just tall enough for thugs and prostitutes to travel the mud trails beneath, unseen. Disgusting smells of waste and human odor came from those undertrails. Those who weren't considered unseemly walked the bridges between buildings, creating a chaotic mess—one in which even Minna could hide.

Unfortunately, it was difficult to hide with those buffoons yelling that she'd escaped.

Residents of Solga's capital—called Rolika for a reason Minna hadn't bothered to learn—scrambled every direction. Some even pushed others over the edge in their panic. *Amusing.* Most of those who weren't guards or slaves wore ridiculously white dress-like clothing that strapped over only one shoulder and left their arms immodestly exposed. The Krowikie would've been aghast at women dressing in such ways. But Minna just shrugged and took pride in making their clothes feel the earth for once. Well, considering the stench wafting from the chasm, their clothes would surely feel more than just earth.

If it had been up to her, Minna would have used the undertrails for her escape. Lady Marzanna wanted a commotion, however, so the goddess would have one.

She crossed a stone bridge over an undertrail no wider than ten strides. This one was clear of the fleeing people, but more importantly, it took her closer to the woman heretics called The Lady. Just the thought of her made Minna dig her nails into her palm, drawing blood.

When they thought themselves at a safe distance, some of the people turned back to gawk. Minna caught glimpses of their horrific outfits out of the corner of her eye and smirked.

Maybe a little more *show then.*

The moment Minna's foot reached the next platform, full of small domiciles, she snapped her fingers. Gasps echoed from the crowd as the bridge creaked. Stone was strong, but as any mistress of ice knew, it was prone to cracks. Add enough moisture to such cracks, freeze them, and then you had one massive fissure. Basic elements, but The Lady had blinded the Solgawi to reality. Not that the other tribes she'd seen had opened their eyes either.

Minna shook her head as the bridge collapsed into the chasm. Screams echoed from it, and she remembered only then that many of the people had fallen in. Perhaps she should've been ashamed by that, but Lady Marzanna was the goddess of winter *and* death. She would appreciate Minna's offering. And if she didn't, at least their cries for help were quite enjoyable.

More guards approached once Minna had crossed a few more chasms, destroying each bridge she passed. No one could tolerate that much attention for long. Oblivion, even The Lady herself cast out her suitors when she was holding court in Rolika's palace, and *she* claimed to be a fertility goddess.

These guards kept their distance with fear ruling their eyes. Minna sighed. Apparently, word spread quicker in this godsforsaken city than she'd anticipated. The Lady was beginning her "Solitude" in the temple, but she would be escorted to a more secure location if they figured out who Minna was.

"Enough have seen," Lady Marzanna whispered. *"Complete your mission quickly, my pet. I have brought you back too many times for you to fail now."*

Death. Minna knew him better than her family. Well, it would be hard for her not to, considering she didn't remember them anymore. Lady Marzanna had said Minna would become less *her* and more *like her goddess* each time she returned from the afterlife. Three deaths later, Minna was just starting to grasp what that meant.

Something jabbed at her.

Right, the insolent guards.

With her mistress's permission to kill more freely, Minna pooled *žityje* in her hands, summoning two ice daggers that she swiftly sent flying into the guards' skulls. They may have wounded her if they hadn't been so hesitant. Too close for comfort.

Comfort wasn't Minna's lot, however. She thrived in the uncanny and unknown. That meant putting herself in… odd… situations— something Lady Marzanna requested often. Today would be chief among them, and Minna's heart raced in excitement.

Her target wasn't far now. With stilts three times taller than the surrounding buildings, The Lady's temple made of wooden posts and endless ivy appeared like a stain upon Rolika's attempt to expel all nature from within the city bounds. How anyone, let alone someone claiming to be a goddess of fertility, could tolerate mounds of refuse filling the trails below, Minna didn't know. Lady Marzanna had once been a goddess of nature, and even now, she believed in its power. Rolika was a rejection of it.

Pathetic.

Wondrous screams met Minna's ears as she crossed the final chasm before the temple. Like a wave crashing against a boat's stern, the guards rushed from its platform before collapsing, pierced by her ice shards. Weak, useless. Why did

The Lady rely so heavily on mortal guards when she claimed to be a goddess? It was as if she *wanted* her precious city to be taken from her.

Some part of Minna remembered mortality. It stunk like Death himself—or more the fear of his inevitable arrival. Service to Lady Marzanna had freed Minna of such feeble worries, but that unruly piece of her mourned sending mortals to the underworld of Nawia. She squashed its dissonance as she pushed aside the ivy hanging from the temple's wooden frame and stepped inside.

Beyond, two rows of wooden pillars lined an intricately woven rug. Hidden within its designs, Minna saw many words in the old tongue: a spell of protection.

So, she didn't leave herself so vulnerable after all…

Minna slipped to the right of the rug and pillars, keeping her channeling ready. Though avoiding the rug's defensive sorcery should've been enough to keep her safe, The Lady would have other protections. Surprisingly, no guards followed her. At least twenty of them lined the walls of hanging vines, watching from a distance. Minna shivered beneath their gaze.

But the guards meant little besides the *žityje* flowing through their souls. So close she could practically feel it merging with her own. Perhaps when she was finished, she'd feed before leaving. It had been far too long.

"I wondered when Marzanna would find me," a sweet voice said from across the temple.

Minna moved toward the voice, calling forth her ice daggers again. The cold stung her hands, but she smiled as she passed the final column.

At the temple's head, standing in a pool of swamp water up to her bare chest with three naked men by her side, was the one they called The Lady. Dark, wet brown hair clung to her wide shoulders and full breasts as she raised her round face to study Minna. Tanned and with eyes as deep as a river, she truly appeared like the fertility goddess she claimed to be—until one saw her skinless back, revealing bloodied organs. Minna knew better than Rolika's mortals. The enormous amount of *žityje* lurking in her target's soul wasn't because she was a goddess.

The Lady was a demon.

2

Kostroma

KOSTROMA SIGHED AS SHE RAN HER FINGERS down the stubbled cheek of the consort who held her in his arms. A shame he would have to die for her. They all did in the end, but she'd lost sorrow for them many lifetimes ago. Her *žityje* had to come from somewhere. Why not willing men?

Usually, she at least had the chance to lie with them first, but Marzanna apparently wanted to take away the little pleasure she had in life. Or, well, death. Kostroma hadn't lived since the gods betrayed her.

"Lady Marzanna didn't need to find you," the ice goddess's pet snarled, stalking toward Kostroma's pool, lined with indigo and yellow-red flowers called Kupalo-da-Miawkas. Yet another reminder of what she'd become. "My queen knows all, Kostroma."

Oh, so she truly does know my name.

Kostroma narrowed her eyes and freed herself from the consort's grasp with a tender kiss upon his cheek. What had he called himself? Wiktor? Bruno? They'd all blurred together after so long. Bless their hearts… Their delectable, *žityje*-filled hearts.

"So, you have come to kill The Lady," she said, gently pushing away the other two consorts who reached for her arm, their eyes glazed over in awe. That much hadn't changed with her fall. "That is ambitious, but what will Marzanna do with you when you fail? Bring your soul back until you forget all but her? Until you know nothing but winter and death, wishing for Nawia's release yet never finding it?"

"You know nothing of Lady Marzanna."

"A child you are." Kostroma scoffed as she emerged from the pool and waved for a consort to bring her robe. "What knowledge can a simple szeptucha claim to hold of the gods, of eternity? You wield the force of winter like a boy does a wooden sword, swinging it at whatever offends you. *You*, little one, know nothing of Marzanna."

She shivered with her skin exposed to the unnaturally cold air of the Czerwiec moon. It was just weeks before the summer solstice. Jaryło and Dziewanna had supposedly killed Marzanna moons ago, yet snow covered everything beyond Rolika, and clusters of a strange, deadly illness had appeared in recent moons. Combined with reports of lands falling fallow and this szeptucha's presence, that could mean only one thing.

"How did she do it?" Kostroma asked as the consort slid the sleeves of an indigo linen robe over her arms. She then shooed him away, leaving its front open. Her foe's discomfort pleased her.

The szeptucha frowned. "Do what?"

Does she even know? Or is Marzanna hiding the truth from her pets as well? Kostroma clicked her tongue. *Typical.*

"Jaryło and Dziewanna," Kostroma continued. "Life hasn't returned since the equinox, so surely your thick-headed goddess did *something* to them." She advanced, studying her prey. This intruder obviously believed herself to be the predator, but nothing could be further from the truth. "Did she kill them too with that Thunderstone dagger Swaróg crafted so long ago? Slit the throat of her lover with the very blade gifted to her at their wedding? And her sister?"

Kostroma grinned and stopped before the girl. Adorable how this szeptucha believed hiding ice daggers within her sleeves would fool someone who'd lived for millennia. Tempting her to strike was half the fun. "Isn't it awful realizing how little you mean to Marzanna?"

That did the trick.

The first blade pierced Kostroma's bare stomach just above the navel—she took this blow with satisfaction. As the second raced toward her head, though, she ducked faster than any mortal. Blood seeped from her wound, but the pain was nothing compared to the *žityje* she'd draw from this szeptucha. A feast far greater than her mortal consorts.

Was the girl *screaming*? She must've been, because a harsh sound slashed at Kostroma's ears as she kicked out the szeptucha's knee, sending her sprawling. Even that didn't stop the piercing noise, and the red-faced girl scrambled to her feet, her teeth bared and her braided hair unwinding.

"You'll die for defying Lady Marzanna's will!"

Kostroma just smirked, extending her arms to the side. Pain stabbed at her fingertips, but she'd felt it a million times as her claws grew rapidly from them. The szeptucha's gaping mouth alone was worth it.

"You're just a miawka!" the Frostmarked hissed. "A lowly demon, not The Lady!"

Ripping the dagger from her stomach, Kostroma laughed. *Žityje* drained from her soul as the wound healed in seconds, but it had been far too long since she'd been forced to use much of it. On this, the szeptucha was right. Kostroma was a swamp demon known as a miawka. What she didn't realize, though, was that Kostroma *craved* the use of her power.

"Oh, my loves," Kostroma called across the temple to her enchanted guards. "I don't believe our visitor knows how to treat a lady."

They charged instantly, their boots striking the wooden floors with a racket as the szeptucha scowled. The temperature dropped. Kostroma's breaths turned to fog, but she'd seen this before. In truth, she didn't even need the guards' help to kill this girl, yet commanding them like the toys they were felt *so* much more fun. She spun away as the szeptucha sent bolts of ice slicing after her. A simple trick.

Though the shards struck down the first few guards, Kostroma and the remaining sixteen remained unharmed. She grinned as they jabbed their spears without her even needing to guide them.

The szeptucha turned to the guards, using her channeling to freeze their legs to the ground and create ice shields that blocked their strikes. Within seconds, they would surely be dead. But Kostroma hadn't needed them to kill Marzanna's assassin, just distract her. She'd never have allowed many of her best pets to die so uselessly, and she definitely wouldn't allow them to take the satisfaction of *her* kill.

Kostroma's claws streaked through the air. The szeptucha saw her advance, but she was no quicker than a mortal. As she encircled herself in a spiked wall of ice, Kostroma leaped to the temple's thatched ceiling, the demon's thrill surging within her. She could taste the *žityje* already.

From above, Kostroma watched her guards stumble away from the ice wall, wounded and frightened. Such battles were never meant for mortals, but they'd done their job. She dropped, and her claws found the szeptucha's throat before the girl could summon another shield.

Blood poured from the wound, and Kostroma caught the szeptucha as she collapsed with rage in her eyes. That glare was all too familiar. It had been a long time since the gods had sent a servant to kill the first miawka——their own accidental creation—but each had held that same visceral hatred of her. Why wouldn't they? To szeptuchy, she was nothing but a demon who claimed to be a goddess. They had no way of knowing the truth.

Kostroma had been a goddess. Once.

The chill vanished as Kostroma knelt over her kill. Marzanna wasn't the one she hated the most, but her soul swelled knowing she'd bested the gods again. Someday, she'd get her revenge. Ruling Rolika as The Lady would do for now. If Marzanna had discovered her secret, however, how long did she truly have until others tried to send her to Oblivion—the only possible end for a demon?

She pushed away those doubts. They could wait. The pool of *žityje* in her victim's heart could not, and her own heart raced as she carved through the szeptucha's ribs with her claws. Once the heart was exposed, she grabbed it eagerly and bit.

Bliss filled her along with the rush of *žityje*. In her many years, she'd never found anything more pleasurable than satisfying the demon's hunger.

Let it starve and it could drive her mad, but it had been centuries since Kostroma had been far from a source of the life force. Devouring a heart as full of it as a szeptucha's was rare. She savored every mouthful.

When she finished, she took a deep breath and examined the melting wall of ice around her. The guards stood attentively, staring at her. They showed no disgust at the blood that coated her fingers and chin, but why would they? Rolika worshipped her. To them, The Lady wasn't a demon. She was a goddess, and a far more merciful one than most.

"Burn the body," she commanded as she retracted her claws. "Marzanna has a nasty knack of bringing back her szeptuchy, and I have no desire to deal with this pest again."

One of the guards bowed. "Yes, my lady."

Kostroma pushed up his chin, examining his strong cheekbones and deep brown eyes. *Yes, him next.* "Find me in my chambers when you are finished."

She kissed his forehead and walked past before he could stutter out a shocked reply. All the men in Rolika sought such an opportunity with her, even though they knew most never returned from her rooms. Such was the lot of a miawka—one far better than most demons in her eyes. At least she could have fun before surrendering to the demon's curse.

Thoughts of the time before the gods' betrayal filled her head as she disrobed and stepped into the warm pool once again. By mortal standards, she'd been only a young woman—a mere infant to a deity. Her father had protected her for so long, fought for her when she was betrayed, but Perun and the others had taken him by then. Simargł, god of the wild flame, was too dangerous they claimed. All Kostroma knew was that she hadn't seen her father since, nor had she met her lover, Kupalo, after she learned the truth about him.

The horrible truth.

Her fingers closed around a Kupalo-da-Miawka flower as the consorts approached. She accepted their tender caress but stared only at the two heads of the flower. One indigo, the other yellow streaked with red. Tears stung her eyes.

What happened to you, brother?

3

Minna

"**Again… Again?** Lady Marzanna saved me. Of-Of course she did. I've always been loyal. Always loyal…"

Familiar, frigid sand stung Minna's cheek and hands as she dug her fingers deep into it, muttering to herself. The Way of Souls had taken her for the fourth time. Or perhaps it was more. It was all a blur in her head. Even her name flickered in and out of her memory—sometimes Minna, sometimes Vida. The thought of the latter made her writhe, bones cracking and joints bending the wrong way. But she felt no pain beyond the sand.

Such was Death's realm.

It was a long time before her body found a form resembling that of a human. Toes remained twisted and her shoulder swung oddly, but it would do. So she rose, taking in the endless landscape before her, its dark masses of flat sand broken only by the flaming Smorodina River. Just strides away, its heat didn't meet her skin, or at least she didn't sense it.

The realm was silent. Neither the eight winds nor the birds reached this desolate place at Nawia's edge, caught between life's suffering and paradise's lies. There was no deceit here, no false promises so common among mortals. No, the only voice that graced this plane was the Lady Marzanna's herself, and each word she spoke was the most beautiful Minna had ever heard.

"You return so soon," the goddess of winter and death hissed. Her voice didn't echo, but it hung on the still air, allowing the weight of her disappointment to linger heavily on Minna's frail body.

Minna groveled, unwilling to look upon her mistress. She was Lady Marzanna's most loyal servant, but she was not worthy. Failure would not please her queen. "I'm sorry, my lady." What was she sorry for this time?

"Pitiful, what little of you remains." Lady Marzanna sighed. A chill ran through Minna as the goddess's breath drifted over her, and with each step of her goddess's feet through the sand, Minna shivered in anticipation of her touch. "Not that you were much when I pulled your corpse from that pond nearly five years ago. A child left to die by the gods. Forgotten. Unneeded. *Unwanted.* But I saw your potential."

Her long, arcing claw touched Minna's collarbone. The szeptucha breathed in sharply, pleasure racing through her as the claw crept up her neck until Lady Marzanna's chilled hand cupped her cheek. She forced Minna to raise her gaze, and the szeptucha gasped when she did.

Minna had forgotten much with her many deaths. That stunning face, though, was burned into her memory. Sharp cheekbones highlighted eyes the color of a freshly frozen river, and midnight hair hung long over her pure white dress. Her lips were thin and light, barely hiding wolf-like teeth that dripped blood. She'd been fed. Good. Lady Marzanna deserved offerings, and she rewarded greatly those who brought them.

"You killed many in my name before Kostroma bested you." The goddess's voice quieted, but its force remained, even in a whisper. "I have feasted well from your gifts."

"I'm glad," Minna replied. "All I live for is to honor you, Lady."

The grip tightened. Minna sputtered at the fingers clutching her throat and claws digging into her jaw.

"Yet you fail me time and time again!" Lady Marzanna spat. Darkness rose from her skin in wisps, circling the pair as her eyes streaked with black. "How many gifts must I grant you until you fulfill that promise I saw? Most others receive only one before I lose faith in them, yet this will be your fourth—*if* I choose to grant you another."

Tears stung Minna's eyes as she grasped her lady's arm, her nails digging into the funeral cloths wrapped up to Marzanna's elbow. "I won't fail again! I swear!"

Marzanna screeched. The sound pierced Minna's skull, and she scrambled back. Too slowly. The goddess's claws raked across her face from temple to nose, sending black blood spewing down her chin. With the cut over her good eye, she struggled to open it, and only the stench of death alerted her to the goddess's second strike.

Minna's thoughts turned to agony as Marzanna gripped her skull, palm over her

Frostmark. It seared as if the goddess had shoved her face into the Smorodina's fiery flow. She pled. She wept. But her lady would not relent, and a force crept through her mind.

I chose this.

Just one moon before, she'd willingly accepted Marzanna's pain over remembering her first life. It had been her third death. The most terrifying yet, as she'd lost control of Vastroth in her defeat, but she'd begged for another chance. To prove herself to her goddess. Yet she'd found death again. She feared what would come of the fifth.

But that worry vanished, drawn away by the growing maw in her mind. Devouring and consuming her memories, her weakness, Marzanna's power coursed through Minna until even recalling her own name became a struggle. Any concept of that girl... Vida... dissolved along with the remnant thoughts of her Krowikie tribe and the vague features of a face she recognized as her sister's. Locations and their names lingered, but they were foreign, strange as she opened her unscarred eye through the pain.

All she saw was her lady's beautiful face through her clawed fingers. *Those memories are lies,* she told herself. *This is all that matters. This is my home.*

"Let me stay," Minna stammered. "I can serve you better at your side!"

Marzanna spun away sharply. "Come, my pet. I have much more planned for you."

Minna's body ached as she forced herself to scramble after her mistress. Blood pooled over her eye and stung her with each blink, but she couldn't stop. Pleasing her goddess gave Minna's life worth. No pain would stop her from serving.

The black sand burned against Minna's twisted, exposed toes. It was as if her body hadn't remembered how to be human, settling instead for a crude depiction that was hardly functional. Her lady offered no help. Nor did she slow for her struggling szeptucha. But that wasn't Lady Marzanna's fault. She was a goddess, and Minna was merely a tool to ensure her eventual reign over Jawia. It was Minna's responsibility to keep pace, not the other way around.

Time dragged on with each agonizing stride. The sea of ashen sand stretched for an eternity along the Smorodina, and sweat stung Minna's open wounds as the flames seemed to draw closer. Some mortal remnant of her mind wished to succumb to the river's pull. Death, true death, lay on the opposing shore, but that was not to be her end. Lady Marzanna would not permit her to rest in Weles's paradise for perished souls. No, only Oblivion would meet her once she lost her lady's favor, so she staggered onward until a faint outline of a building appeared in the dull firelight.

Lady Marzanna stopped at the building's threshold, her hand on its splintered wooden door. Sleek obsidian formed the building's walls and flat roof. No windows offered a view inside. Despite its sheen, no reflection appeared upon the exterior, and light itself bent around them, as if sucked in by their emptiness. All except the door.

"Few step foot upon these sands and live to speak of them," the death goddess said, her voice pulled away by some unseen force. "None return from Death's dungeon."

She dragged her claws down the door. A thin layer peeled with them, the scratching piercing Minna's mind and deafening her to all else. The claw marks joined dozens of symbols etched into the wood as Lady Marzanna whispered in the old tongue, "*Mini.*" Pass.

The symbol she'd carved flashed ice-blue before vanishing with all the other marks. An iron knocker replaced them. Six green dragon heads held its bar, which Lady Marzanna rang against the door thrice.

Minna didn't breathe as the door creaked open, but no one was on the other side. "My lady, what is this place?" she asked as she fell to her knees.

But Lady Marzanna simply stepped into the darkness beyond, curling one clawed finger to signal for her szeptucha to follow. So she did. Slowly, painfully, Minna dragged herself to the threshold, but hesitated before crossing. Superstitions abounded among many tribes about entering a building unwelcomed, particularly for the undead like her. Why did that give her pause? Those tribes weren't hers, right?

She bit her cheek and pushed on as the air cooled beyond the doorway. An obsidian floor replaced the sand here. To the right and left, it extended beyond her sight, but torches lined the path before her. Down. A deep red carpet covered the steps—so she thought.

As Lady Marzanna's dress slid over each, scarlet crept up the fabric, and the wet, sticky feeling beneath Minna's feet was far too familiar. She'd sacrificed enough mortals to recognize blood by the smell alone. The stale air had given no hint, but there was no other explanation for the thick liquid dripping off each ledge.

Minna just continued on after her mistress. The blood made every step perilously slippery, but the goddess's radiant glow filled her gaze. She walked in a trance. Though her feet remained mangled and her joints twisted, she no longer stumbled. Lady Marzanna was strong, so she would be too. This was why she was the favored szeptucha. This was why death meant nothing to her. As long as Lady Marzanna loved her, she was free.

Minna's body throbbed by the time they reached the stairs' end. Another faint prick of mortality that joined with her facial wounds. She raised an unsteady hand to her temple, then held it before her to see the darkness that oozed from her skin.

Her heart beats within me. Her blood pulses through my veins.

Lady Marzanna gave her a fanged smile and pointed ahead, where a square of flames entrapped a figure in the center of the large, otherwise empty room. No light entered the space. Only the constant glow of the prison fires revealed the kneeling man within, and his blond hair seemed to burn as he stared at Minna with black eyes.

"This one reeks of death," he said, his voice as cold as frost. "There's something else, though, and I think I know why you brought her here."

"Silence, Kupalo," Lady Marzanna commanded.

The man spasmed, clutching at his throat but failing to even choke. His arching brows and bared teeth said enough, and fangs longer than even Lady Marzanna's glinted in the firelight. They were stained red.

Minna looked to her goddess. "The brother. Kostroma searches for him."

"Yes," she replied with the *S* carrying through the room. "Kostroma has spent many years hoping to reunite with her twin, but she is too blind to see that he, too, became a demon after their suicides."

"But they deserve death for opposing you."

"The deaths I speak of were long ago." Lady Marzanna approached the flames, locking eyes upon Kupalo and raising her hand. Ice danced at each finger. "I have told you of the deceit that led to my marriage to my own twin, but Jaryło and I tried to love for a time. Kostroma and Kupalo did not."

"Noc Kupały…"

Memories slipped into Minna's mind. Another person's surely, as they showed festivals around the summer solstice, girls adorning wreaths and laughing as boys caught them in the river. She'd never had a tribe. Marzanna had always guided her, even before... Before what? She couldn't remember her initiation as a Frostmarked szeptucha. Or her childhood. Or...

Her hand twitched, and when she blinked away the intrusive thoughts, Kupalo was grinning at her. It was a knowing gaze. Minna hated it.

"Many tribes named their solstice festival in remembrance of the twins' tale," Lady Marzanna continued, circling the fire. "Each changes how their demise came to be, but the crucial element remains the same: The gods tricked them. When the twins were mere children, the gods led them to a grove where Alkonost and Sirin sang. Sisters with beautiful female heads and the bodies of birds, each enchanted one of the twins. Little did they know that the Sirin steals those who hear her song, and she took Kupalo to Nawia."

"I remember the rest of the story," Minna replied. Curiosity pushed her closer, and she studied the demon as she spoke. "Kostroma taunted the gods years later on the solstice, so they threw the flower crown from her head and into a river. Kupalo found it when he returned to Jawia. Tradition forced them to marry, but the gods didn't reveal they were siblings until afterward. So they killed themselves."

Lady Marzanna stopped on the opposite side of Kupalo. "Sounds familiar, does it not? The gods manipulating the youngest of their kind and tricking them into marriage, only for it to end with their corruption?"

"My Lady, then why did you ask me to kill her?"

"To bring her into my domain."

Ice shot from the goddess's hands, dousing the nearest of the flames as Kupalo spun to meet his captor. He staggered to his feet, but he never got the chance to strike.

"Never attack your lady," Lady Marzanna instructed with a hand out toward him. Then she closed the fist.

Kupalo dropped to his knees again, a symbol burning its way across his back. Marzanna's Frostmark. The X crossed at each end glowed brighter and brighter as the fallen god opened his mouth to scream, but no sound came. He followed Lady Marzanna. Not out of the righteous worship that fueled Minna's soul, but out of compulsion. This close, her Frostmark allowed her to command him as she wished. That brought a smile to Minna's face.

The goddess mirrored her szeptucha's grin. "If you cannot kill the miawka, then tell her I have her brother. Tell her we are very much the same, and that I have what it takes to free her father, to grant her the revenge that we both seek against the gods."

"Her father?" Minna stepped to the edge of the remaining fires. "Who?"

"Simargł. The lord of the flames. The husband of the night." Lady Marzanna grabbed Kupalo by his hair and dragged him to Minna. The fire left no marks upon her skin, and she towered over her pet as she took Minna's cheek. "Together, we will devour the gods."

4

Kostroma

THE LADY SAT UPON SOLGA'S THRONE OF IRON, leaning on her knees as she stared down at the gathered warriors before her. Soldiers. Generals. Scouts. They all gave her the same disappointing news.

"What use are you if you cannot find a single man?" she asked sharply.

Commander Timo knelt on one knee before her with his head bowed. Out of his usual chain mail, the bulky, long-haired man looked far too vulnerable for a warrior whose kill count numbered nearly a thousand. The boar pelts hung over his tunic were meant to honor him, but to Kostroma, they made him look soft. He ran his scarred left hand through his light brown beard. The ring finger was missing, leaving a gruesome stump just below the knuckle.

"It is easy to find an army, my lady," he said in a gruff voice. "One man is far more difficult."

Kostroma shot to her feet. Tufts of hair curled before her ears, the rest of it tucked back over a dress of shimmering green that flowed along the stone steps before the throne. Her advisors claimed it was immodest for the queen to wear gowns exposing her shoulders and neck, but she liked how it disarmed the men who confronted her. Not that it took much effort with her combined miawka allure and remnant powers as a fertility goddess.

"I do not care about Krowikie forces!"

Her voice carried on through the room, barely dampened by the spiraled fabrics covering the tall windows along the side walls. Luxuries created vulnerabilities that the gods' assassins had taken advantage of more than once. Mortals longed for it, though. They needed beautiful things around their leaders. If their queen could have such things, then someday they too could aspire for greater. All of it meant nothing to Kostroma. Comfort bred laxness, and laxness would delay her plans.

No, she didn't need to be surrounded by beauty. She needed revenge. Until then, pleasure and survival would do. It was only a matter of time until her scouts found Kupalo. Surely…

The warriors wavered beneath her fury. Her attendants knew better than to show fear around her, as she would never harm them, but these men relied on the rumors of The Lady. Rumors Kostroma had spent countless hours fostering. They allowed her to mold these warriors to her will—all but Timo.

"We search for your brother with each passing day, my lady, but we must act," the commander replied with no weakness in his voice. He was careful not to mention Dadźbóg, god of the sun, as many less familiar with The Lady would have. "Raids from Krowik only allow the villagers to grow more restless. Trarey, Volkbirn, and Grimden all lost people and resources. They want blood. If it's not Krowikie, it'll be yours."

The gall of men.

Kostroma's footfalls echoed as she descended the six steps to Timo. Such challenging rhetoric was worthy of punishment for even the commander of the Solgawi army. Unlike the rest of his men, Timo had resisted her sway, and that made him all the more frustrating… and fascinating.

"What do a few farmhands mean compared to a war among the gods?" she spoke down to him. "Marzanna sent a szeptucha because I am the last one standing in her way, but I am but one goddess. I need Kupalo to help me free my father."

"And if he doesn't want to be found?"

The smack stung Kostroma's knuckles, but it was the least enforcement she could offer. A woman's backhand. Timo had taken far worse and would understand that a queen must rule with authority.

"Find him," Kostroma finished, turning away from the petitioners. Her dress and hair covered the skinless part of her back that exposed the organs beneath, but even when revealed, most men were too blinded by her miawka seductions. Those that resisted spread rumors that made her courtiers fear her back as much as her glare. It marked her as a beast—a true title that she would cut out the tongue of anyone who spoke.

Timo's leather boots dragged across the stone as he stood. A moment passed before he bowed, his deep blue cape attached at the collar swooshing with the motion. Even with the hesitation, Kostroma hadn't feared insubordination from him. The commander knew his place, and he would do his duty whether he liked it or not. If only all the warriors were so compliant.

The hall emptied in moments. Despite the warriors' lingering lustful gazes, they fled their commanders' rage quickly.

Kostroma returned to her throne, her hall now empty except for her servants and a few guards. She welcomed the silence. Ruling a queendom as large as Solga took immense effort, and though she left most decisions to advisors who actually cared about the realm, she tired. Marzanna's ridiculous rebellion should have offered her a chance to free her father while the gods were distracted. Instead, she wallowed away in a stupid demonic body without Kupalo to help.

Stop thinking like a child, she told herself.

It had been centuries since she'd become a demon. In that time, she'd never seen her brother again, but she had never lost hope of finding him. Until now.

Her plan had seemed infallible all those years ago, when she'd first set her sights on Rolika's palace. Solga had held the most powerful mortal army in all of Jawia before Marzanna gave Koschei the Deathless command of her Horde. It didn't matter. No men were enough to find Kupalo, and she was certain that even the Horde probably would've failed. She tapped her foot.

What if they hadn't?

At that thought, the throne room doors opened, tearing the queen from her thoughts. Mortals were far too often a nuisance. Lately, however, so was her mind, and she sighed in relief at the distraction.

"Who approaches The Lady?" her attendant asked. A tall thin man in a tailed coat woven with multicolored fabrics, he had a voice high enough to make one's ears ring. Kostroma affectionately referred to him as Mouse.

The visitor's chest rose and fell rapidly as he dropped to a knee. He wore the studded leather armor of lower ranked warriors, and no short sword filled the sheath at his hip. Mouse's question was a formality, as the guards outside would have questioned the man, but the palace's rules regarding weapons were not. No one except Kostroma's personal guard entered the throne room armed. Unless they wanted to be her next feast, of course.

"Robert, son of Torsten," the visitor huffed. Sweat dripped from his dirtied brow. Who was this man? A dungeon guard? A warden whipping the slaves who built Rolika's mighty walls?

Curiosity pulled Kostroma to break custom. "And what brings you here, Robert, son of

Torsten?" she asked, ignoring Mouse's squeak. Whatever it was, it had to be interesting if the guards had allowed him through. Many of her people petitioned for her attention daily, but she didn't have time for the requests of peasants. They would all either die from starvation or slaughter unless she devoted her entire attention to freeing her father.

"The channeler, my lady," Robert mumbled, shaking. "We threw her onto the pyre, but she just stood up. Never seen anything like it. Sliced two good men's necks before we got her."

Now this *is fun.*

Kostroma grinned and dug her fingers into the throne's armrests. She kept her claws hidden before most mortals, but in her excitement, she allowed them to emerge for a moment, scraping across the stone and leaving gorges behind. "Bring her to me."

A cough came from her right, and a balding man emerged from the shadows in the corner. He wore a sweeping indigo robe strapped over one shoulder. Vines hung from his hands, holding up a wooden bowl filled with burning melilot flowers to purify the room. A charade, but one Kostroma needed to uphold her image as a goddess.

"It is unwise to bring one so tainted into your holy presence, my lady," the man said with all the strength of a young warrior. "She has already made one attempt on your life."

The Lady scowled. "I need not be reminded of that, Luca. Your place is as my priest, not as king. You will not speak your opinion unless I ask for it." Then she turned her attention back to Robert, raising her now clawless fingers. "Bring the szeptucha. Let us see the dead walk."

The guardsman stumbled as he stood, then bowed. "Yes, my lady."

Each moment after allowed Kostroma's anticipation to swell. It was rare for her to find a match, let alone one that returned after death. This szeptucha meant something to Marzanna, and that would make torturing the goddess's pet oh so sweet. Maybe she'd even have the honor of being The Lady's meal yet again. Kostroma licked her teeth at the thought of *żityje*.

Her heart jumped when the doors dragged open, revealing the one-eyed witch who'd dared to attack her days before. Torn brown rags fell over the girl's body and dark gouges crossed above and below her good eye. She no longer stood like a confident channeler, instead curling over with her mangled brown hair clinging wet to her face and neck. The room chilled at her presence.

In Kostroma's chest, a new fire burned.

"Either your goddess wishes for you to suffer," she said, standing and staring down at her foe, "or she sent you for a reason other than dueling. Though, if you wish to face me again, I would not deny myself the taste of your flesh."

Slowly, she descended the steps and plucked a Kupalo-da-Miawka flower from the pot at the bottom. Indigo for her. Yellow streaked in red for Kupalo. The gods believed a plant could make right what they'd done, but it was just another reminder of what Kostroma had lost. She had fallen. She would never again be a goddess at her mother and father's sides. So she'd rid Prawia of them all.

"Quiet now?" she asked. "Hmm. I expected more after you interrupted me so rudely at my temple."

Eyes of black met her. Demonic blood seeped from them and trickled down the szeptucha's pale face, dripping onto her parted lips. "Your temple stains the living realm," the girl said, "but Lady Marzanna is merciful. I am called Minna, and she has gifted me new life. Now, she gifts you a new chance."

Kostroma hissed and stormed to Minna, closing her free hand around her neck. She wished to squeeze more than anything. Not yet. "I have seen what it means to receive gifts from the gods. Nothing better than curses."

Minna cackled. "You're desperate, weak." She snatched Kostroma's wrist, but as the guards moved to strike, The Lady signaled for them to stop.

"I have waited a thousand years to see my brother again, to embrace my father. What do you know of desperation, mortal? Do you even remember your own family?"

More laughter, yet something flickered behind the szeptucha's madness. It disappeared before Kostroma could understand. "Lady Marzanna is my mother, my sister, my everything. I need nothing of this realm."

"She uses you, child." Kostroma released her and stepped away, looking from Minna to the flower. An ache filled her. Pain, old and buried. "I'd free you from that burden, but I fear she would only return you to this broken land with less of your soul than before. I wonder how much remains even now."

"You mock her, but she has what you want."

The flower slipped from Kostroma's fingers. "No! You lie!"

Minna's laughs echoed through the hall, haunting Kostroma as she backed away, but there was no escape. She saw the truth on the szeptucha's face, heard it in her words. "Submit to her will and relinquish the throne of Solga to me, and then Kupalo is yours. You can have your brother. Then Lady Marzanna will have your father."

"We won't serve her!"

The Frostmark glowed upon Minna's eye as she bared her teeth. "Kupalo already does. Simargł will too! He'll bring fire to the frozen realm and burn all who defy Lady Marzanna. Czarnobóg and Simargł will consume Jawia together. They will follow the true goddess, and all the false ones will fall."

Kostroma's breaths weakened. She spun away, claws digging into her palms. It couldn't be true! Kupalo would never serve the goddess of winter and death. He would have fought until his last breath to be free, and he *would* reunite with her. They would free their father together—not with Marzanna or any dragon, no matter how powerful.

"Take her to one of the spare rooms," she said to the guards over her shoulder. "Strap her down and make a circle around her with leaves of a linden tree. Fill the room with melilot smoke, and if she resists, do not allow her to leave. Marzanna has sent her as a messenger. As long as I consider the offer, she is a hostile envoy."

Kostroma circled one of the stone pillars. A small shield between her and Minna. It gave her time to collect herself as the guards dragged the witch out.

"You'll regret this!" Minna shrieked. "Your brother will never see Jawia's light if you resist Lady Marzanna!"

"Then neither shall you."

Minna's screams rang through the hall, even once the doors closed behind her. They split Kostroma's ears and pierced her mind. All she saw was her lost brother's face. All she smelled were the flowers of the spring blooms they spent together. She'd thought she had everything, but it was a lie, and as she slipped away to her chambers, she wondered if she would ever know who she truly was.

Goddess. Demon. Lady. Nothing.

I'll free you, Brother. With my last breath, I will hold you, and we will never let them tear us apart again.

5

Kupalo

FIRE AND ICE. Blood and pain.

Every line of Marzanna's Frostmark seared across Kupalo's back as he knelt amid a pool of black blood. His blood. Sorcerous fire illuminated the pool and stung his wounds. Endless.

Time had become fluid ever since the winter goddess captured him, and he fell in and out of a daze. Visions filled those gaps. Of Simargł and Kupalnitsa's godly parentage. Of Kostroma's excitement when she'd heard the songs of Alkonost and the Sirin. Of her fear when the monstrous woman-headed bird dragged him to the depths of Nawia, where Weles tried to claim him. The years after his return to Jawia were a blur.

Except his death.

He remembered standing on that cliff edge, staring down at the rushing river below with Perun's words whispering through his mind. *"She's your twin, Kupalo. She mocked us, so we gave her to you."*

Tears had streamed down his face, but he lacked the strength to wipe them away. It didn't matter. All he'd loved, all he'd known, had been lost. He was a god, but his life meant nothing. He wanted no more of it.

Yet, no matter how hard he pushed, he couldn't step over the ledge. Whether out of doubt or some primal instinct to survive, he stood rooted to the spot. The resistance grew with each passing moment, and his fear grew with it. Not fear for himself. No, he didn't care about his own fate. He feared what would happen if he was too afraid to jump, if Kostroma found Nawia without him and suffered alone while he lived on like a coward.

The years since had passed so quickly. Despite his body's stubbornness, he had leapt from that cliff, only to find that his soul would never find Nawia or his twin. He'd been a god then. That moment had turned him into something else.

Kupalo ran his tongue over his fangs. Being an upiór gave him a hunger greater than mortals or even gods could understand. Demons came in many forms, but surely he'd become one of the most frightening types. Once, he had lived in fear of beings more powerful than him.

Now it was he whom they feared.

"Don't follow her," he muttered to himself. "Koska, find a way to free Father without me."

His words carried through the dark stone room. Marzanna needed no guards to trap him here, as the fire square alone would maim him if he were to flee, and even more sorcery waited beyond. This was a prison worthy of a god. There would be no escape unless his sister fought her way into Marzanna's realm at Nawia's edge. He prayed to his distant mother, Kupalnitsa, that she didn't try.

The Frostmark flared again, sending him sprawling on his chest. He shuddered with each breath. What had Marzanna made him? As the fallen god of summer and peace, he had *some* power that remained in his demonic form, but couldn't even wipe the sweat from his brow. Summer meant nothing now. And he hadn't felt peace in centuries.

Thoughts intruded in his mind. Strange, they whispered in a hundred tongues, yet he understood them all. *"You will rise from this dungeon, my pet. The living realm shall soon be ours, and then we will set our sights on Prawia. You can still Ascend. You can still have your birthright."*

Kupalo lost control of his body. His prison flashed by him, then blackness that only faded when he collapsed in the center of a muddied pathway filled with refuse. Buildings of wood and stone rose above with smoke spiraling to the sky. Hundreds of people dressed in fine clothes crossed bridges between them, just out of reach, yet none bothered to spare him a glance.

"The powerful miss what lurks in their shadows," the voices continued. Kupalo recognized them as Marzanna's, but he no longer carried resentment toward them. Instead, the words drew him in, and he found himself *wanting* to listen. *"They are like the lords of Prawia who mock us both. Let us show them the cost of their pride..."*

Mud caked Kupalo's hands and feet as he scrambled on all fours to the base of one of the buildings. Wooden stilts held up each of the platform's corners, and angled beams connected each to the center, beneath which a bird huddled over its eggs. A small brown nightjar. Many tribes called the birds messengers from the gods of Prawia around the summer solstice. He had no idea what time of year it was anymore, especially with Marzanna's cold gripping Jawia, but it didn't matter. The nightjar had come from Perun's realm—Kupalo hated it.

With each step he took, the bird grew more restless, chirping out its warning call, but he wasn't afraid of a bird. He would've shown it mercy once. Now, hunger for *žityje* consumed him. To feast upon anything that could replenish his demonic soul.

He lunged with a snarl. The nightjar flapped its wings, but only a lightning chała could beat an upiór's speed. Kupalo's claws ripped through the bird's frail body, sending crimson spraying over his shirtless torso. The bird hadn't even the chance to cry.

Red filled Kupalo's vision as he devoured the small bird. Starting with the heart, he drained it of all blood and relished at how easy his fangs made ripping flesh. His own heart raced with the thrill of the hunt, of his feast. One bird couldn't satisfy his hunger.

He needed more.

The eggs followed so quickly that, once finished, he couldn't remember eating them. He crouched amid the bird bones and eggshells with blood covering his fingers. Each kill swelled his muscles and increased his height, but his mind turned forward. What he'd consumed no longer mattered. Only what happened next.

Scuffling came from nearby. Kupalo stiffened, scanning the support beams with his clawed fingers still curled before him. The cold stung his skin in the silence that followed, as only his legs, covered in torn linen trousers, offered any warmth. When the Frostmarked pulsed on his back, though, a raging fire burned through his veins.

Movement caught his eye. Slight, but he grinned as he fixed his gaze on the shadows near the far support beam. Huddling amid the cobwebs and dumped excrement were two teenage boys.

"Stay," his raspy, alien voice said.

They watched Kupalo with beady eyes as he crept closer. Muck coated their light skin and brown hair, making them look as much demons as him. Their loose, simple tunics and trousers were so ragged that more flesh was visible than fabric where they were supposed to cover.

The taller of the two put himself between Kupalo and the other. "Killed the bird. Why?"

"Hungry."

"We all are, but that was ours. Raised 'er. Fed 'er." Metal suddenly glinted in the teen's hand. "You'll regret it!"

The fight was hardly fair, but fairness had no place in Kupalo's mind now. Mere seconds passed between the teen pulling the blade and both his and his brother's blood pouring from their slit throats. Blood Kupalo desperately needed.

So he drank greedily. He tore their hearts from their chests, sucking them dry and then finishing what remained in their veins.

When he finished, the voice returned.

"Pull yourself from the mud and rise, my pet. You have tasted flesh. Now find your sister. Show her what you truly are."

Kupalo smiled at his mistress's voice. Unleashed, he could feed until his soul overflowed with glorious *žityje*, and the command echoed through his head as he dug his claws into the support beam and climbed. Toward the prideful. Toward the light.

Toward his feast.

6

Kostroma

Heavy snow blanketed the platforms and trails of Rolika as Kostroma walked beneath the midnight moon. Few people ever crossed the maze of bridges at night, and none did so during blizzards like this. None but The Lady.

Alone or not, Kostroma tugged on the hood of her fur-lined cloak. She normally appeared in public with an array of guards and well-dressed attendants, but tonight was different. The reappearance of Marzanna's szeptucha had changed everything. Kupalo was alive and in the goddess's hands. To take what she'd wanted for centuries, Kostroma had to surrender her queendom and father to Marzanna's will. A terrible choice, but she found herself too tempted in the palace.

So she walked.

Night had always been more familiar than Dadźbóg's brutal day. It was her mother's domain and kinder to her demonic soul, but it was also a time of solitude, reflection. With generals, advisors, priests, and peasants all seeking her, she rarely had the chance to think. Not that she'd been bothered by the constant attention until now.

Strands of her hair slipped free from the hood, fluttering across her nose as she reached one of the bridges her guards claimed Minna had destroyed days before. Hundreds of pounds of stone lay in the ravine. It was an inconvenience at worst. More annoying was that it was taking the slaves so long to even move the rubble. Not only was the construction of the wall proceeding far too slowly to halt the inevitable arrival of the Frostmarked Horde, but now Marzanna was also determined to waste Rolika's resources on bridge reconstruction.

Kostroma scoffed at herself. *Look at me, worrying about bridges and walls. I've become boring.* Luckily, people's infatuations with her weren't because of her personality.

She crossed her arms, tucking each hand up the opposite sleeve. It had been foolish not to bring gloves, but this walk had been a hasty need—one that had carried on for far too long. Consorts awaited her in her chambers. So, too, did the melilot incense she'd requested from Luca in hopes it would help her contact her mother. Hours of thought hadn't made her look forward to either, though, and she didn't know which goddess she feared more: Marzanna or Kupalnitsa.

Her return route to the palace was more direct than her wandering one through the residential districts near the Avka River. She'd nearly made a complete loop through the southern half of the city.

Less soot from the blacksmiths covered the wood and stone here, and there were still enough trees sprouting from the undertrails to remind her nature still existed. Scouts from the east claimed that winter had taken everything beyond the regions directly bordering Rolika. Plants still held their leaves here. Hunters had not ceased returning to the city with deer and boar. Her people attributed this to Kostroma as their goddess, but she questioned whether their belief was folly or fact. Rarely, commoners could have important insights that even an ancient being like her missed. But she was a miawka, her godly powers distant. How was she still channeling nature like Dziewanna?

An eerie feeling slowed her as she neared the center market. A large wooden platform, dozens of shops filled it, creating six narrow alleys that followed the sun's path to ensure shadows never allowed thieves to steal within. During the day at least.

With only the light of the waxing moon to guide her, Kostroma wandered down the second of the alleys. Her favorite bakery was here. A small place, it was smushed on either side by expensive jewelers with wares from the Anvoranie City-States and plunder captured during the last war with Krowik. She could almost smell the warm bread as she sneered at the necklaces and bracelets for rich folk who believed themselves greater than other mortals.

It was here that the creature found her.

She saw the movement out of the corner of her eye, but it darted quicker than her claws. They grew from her fingertips instantly, slashing and stabbing as she followed her foe. Each missed strike deepened her frustration.

Sweat beaded on Kostroma's brow by the time the creature slowed enough for her to get a look. Light-skinned with the blackened veins of the most lost demons, his shirtless torso was muscled. He had uncut blond hair and round cheeks that pushed out his full lips. An odd face for a warrior, as if he were a child who'd never grown up.

"What are you?" she asked the demon, her back curled as she readied her next foray.

He shouldn't have been this difficult to fight. Miawki were master huntresses. Mortal men stood no chance against their allure and aggressive speed when they drew too close, and most demons struggled to last more than a moment in melee against one as powerful as Kostroma. What was this beast to resist her?

A fanged grin replied as the demon cocked his head.

"Why are you here?" Kostroma insisted. By avoiding her flurry of attacks, the demon had turned his back to expose the massive Frostmark emblazoned on it. She'd had enough of Marzanna's tricks.

"You've changed, dear Koska."

That voice…

Kostroma snarled and lunged, pinning him to the bakery door. He didn't resist, and as she stared at him, memories rushed through her mind so quickly she could barely breathe.

Hundreds of years had passed. Could this really be him? This Frostmarked, her brother? Her lover?

"You lie!" she snapped. Tears threatened her eyes, and she hated herself for them. Weakness she couldn't afford. "Kupalo would never take winter's mark!"

His eyes were strange, unfamiliar as he looked back at her. "Not willingly, at first. She has shown me what I am capable of, how I can save Father with her, with you."

"Don't dare speak his name!"

"I… I…" he coughed with her forearm pressed to his throat. Some part of her believed him, but she drowned that hope.

"You left me!" She released him before arcing her claws down his cheek, already reddened with dried blood. "Mother wouldn't even talk to me without you. She blamed us for Father's rage, and then you left me too. Kupek, you were all I had!"

Her tears betrayed her. She backed away, shaking her head at the demon who claimed to be Kupalo. In his face, he saw the man she'd loved. In his voice, she heard the twin she'd spent every childhood moment with. But it couldn't be him. It couldn't!

So she ran to the palace.

Every bit of her demonic speed carried her tired, numb body across platforms and over bridges until her lungs burned. She never looked back. That eerie sensation subsided quickly, but some part of her wondered if he'd followed. That beast. That imposter.

Soon, the palace came into sight. Its gray stone walls were mismatched and uneven, but they shimmered silver in the moonlight. Some would've called its three-halled structure a work of art, but it was a stain in Kostroma's eyes. All of Rolika destroyed nature's will. The palace went further, devouring it and pretending it had some splendor that could match the mountains and swamps. Mortals were blind.

Four guards stood at the stone bridge leading to the palace's expansive platform. They wore the chain mail of Solga's most experienced warriors, as they guarded The Lady herself, but they looked like nothing more than idiotic drunkards to her. She'd seen what these men wanted, how useless they were against any sorcery or demonic threat. In truth, *they* needed protecting from *her*.

"Turn back, woman," the first of them demanded, his hand on his blade's hilt.

Kostroma rolled her eyes and lowered her hood. She hoped her tears had dried enough to not be visible by now. The last thing she needed was to explain to her servants why she'd been crying while beyond the palace without a guard.

The guards turned into a stumbling mess. Each dropped to a knee, apologies escaping their lips like one would flee a żmij dragon—and she was certain they would flee Marzanna's dragon if the rumors of Czarnobóg's return were true. She gave them a royal nod and waved for them to stand. Desperate to get inside and away from the demon in the market, she didn't wait for them to offer an escort. Swiftness was a virtue. Ironically, men with such short lives often lacked it.

Her gaze rose from the palace to the enormous wall rising behind it. A paranoid act, she'd ordered the wall built a year before in hopes of protecting herself from the gods, but even an endless flood of slave labor had not kept its completion on schedule. The Horde was ravaging Krowik. Solga would be next, and Marzanna would not hesitate to ensure Kostroma suffered for defying her.

What am I doing here?

Kostroma sighed and laid a hand on the palace doors, hesitating before pushing them open. She'd asked herself that question countless times since she coerced her way to the throne, and with her brother's voice echoing in her mind, her reign felt more pitiful than ever. What use was it? If Kupalo truly had been turned by the winter goddess, everything she'd done had been for naught. Now she fled him. Her mind knew it was foolish, but her chest seized with every breath.

No, she couldn't see him again. Not like that. *Then how?*

Servants scurried about the entrance hall, its long indigo carpet leading straight toward the throne room as arched doorways on either side marked the way to the other wings: left for the sleeping chambers and right for the guards' training grounds and barracks. Cloudy windows of triangular glass rose to a point at the ceiling's peak. Visitors often told her the light shining through it at midday was like bathing in Prawia itself. They meant it as a compliment, but she didn't take it as one.

Tonight, moonlight slipped through those same windows to the far end of the hall. Only the torches lining the walls and two columns on either side of the rug pushed back the darkness near the main doors. This let Kostroma stay in the shadows as she skirted toward the south hall. Each movement made her twitch, her imagination picturing Kupalo's demonic form in the darkness.

She yelped as a hand touched her arm.

"Lady Kostroma," a serving maid, Juliana, whispered. Her button nose, tight eyes, and widow's peak made her face seem far too large. The girl was a punctual, quiet servant that Kostroma had no will to lose.

"What is it?" The Lady replied with her posture straightened. She'd flinched, but Juliana knew better than to question her.

They entered the narrow hallway, and the girl waited until any guards were out of earshot before replying, "The consorts are ready in your chambers." She pursed her lips but said no more.

"Speak, child." Aggression slipped into her voice. Sloppy. She hadn't become The Lady by barking at serving girls who were only trying to help.

"I…" Juliana held her hands to her chest before taking a sharp breath. "I overheard the prisoner talking to her guards. They seemed… accepting… of her words, and then they went silent."

That gave Kostroma pause as they stopped at the door to her chambers. She ran her thumb over her fingers, forcing herself to think like a queen, not a girl who'd just seen her long-lost brother. Minna was a szeptucha spy. She was dangerous, but she was also an asset if Kostroma could get her to reveal more about Marzanna's plan.

She wants me to be her ally, to surrender to Marzanna so Father will serve her too. A game. I can play a game.

Kostroma smiled at the serving girl. "Thank you for your discretion. I will check on the prisoner. Please deliver a message to Guard Captain Mikael, informing him that no one else is to enter her chambers until I am finished with her."

"Oh, yes." The girl's eyes widened. "I mean, yes, my lady."

"And send the consorts away as well. I won't be needing them this evening."

"You… You want them sent away? My lady, if I may, you never—"

"You may not."

Juliana blushed and bowed. "Of course."

With Juliana's retreating footsteps echoing through the hall, barely muffled by the thin rug, Kostroma turned her attention to the door closest to the entrance hall. It was usually for honored guests. Prisoners had their places in the dungeon, but Minna was different. *Play the game.*

She forced away her fear as she opened the door and entered the mist filled room. The heavy smell of melilot overwhelmed her, but that had been the intent in dulling the szeptucha's power. Apparently, that hadn't worked.

"I should've expected this," she muttered, staring down at the three bodies scattered about the room. Hazy looks filled their eyes, and each held a bloodied blade she assumed they'd used to slit their own throats. "You serve the mistress of death."

"They were not yours in their final moments, *Lady*," Minna replied from her position on the bed. "The true goddess has spoken to them, and they will serve her well in death."

At that last word, each of the corpses released a groan. Blood still seeped from their wounds, but they rose nonetheless and took their positions along the wall. Their gazes were empty. She'd barred the servants from starting a fire for Minna, but their breaths did not fog the frigid air.

Minna sat up in the bed, and Kostroma saw then that her arm restraints had not been broken. That was unexpected. She was a szeptucha capable of far more than breaking iron shackles, even under melilot's sway. These undead guards, though, were far more concerning.

"Ready to speak?" Minna asked. "Or will my lady feast more tonight?"

7

Minna

MINNA GRINNED FROM THE BED in the middle of the room. She'd allowed the guards to leave her tied down until Kostroma inevitably arrived, but iron shackles were little use against her channeling. Extending her fingers, she covered them in a layer of ice that froze the metal until it cracked. Then she flung her legs over the bed's side.

"Restraint, interesting," she said to The Lady, rubbing her wrists. Reddened and irritated, but nothing to a szeptucha. "I'd expected you to attack by now."

"We have fought already," Kostroma replied. The melilot smoke swirled around the miawka, and her hands flexed with sharp claws extending from them. "Yet you returned to give me an offer from Marzanna—one you seem keen to break by manipulating my guards."

Minna cocked her head. "So you have considered it? I wonder if your brother had anything to do with that…" A snarl answered her, and she laughed. "Lady Marzanna foresees all. Divination is not her realm, but she knows us better than we know ourselves. Even you."

"Stop preaching to me."

"Why? Because the mighty Lady of Rolika is afraid?"

Kostroma approached, standing over her and holding up a clawed hand. "I'm not afraid of you or your goddess. All I want is my brother back."

Minna stood to meet her. They were nearly close enough for their noses to touch, and she grinned at the smell of sweat over Kostroma's usual perfumes. "Kupalo is yours if you agree. Free Simargł and leave him under Lady Marzanna's control, then go free with your twin. We both know you want to be rid of this mortal city anyway."

"What use is freeing my father only for him then to be imprisoned by yet another goddess?"

Minna stepped even closer, taking Kostroma's hands. They were soft for a vicious demon. "Not imprisoned, unchained," she breathed. The

Lady's blue eyes swam with gray, but she didn't pull away at Minna's sudden tenderness. "That is Lady Marzanna's promise for each of us. To release us from the chains Jaryło, Perun, Weles, Swaróg, Strzybóg, and all the gods have placed around our necks. They control the Three Realms. Don't you want to be free of them?"

Brows furrowed, Kostroma studied her. "What are you doing? Why does Marzanna need Simargł if she has Czarnobóg? Jawia is practically hers already, and the gods have been split for centuries with Weles warring against Perun and Swaróg."

"The winter takes the living realm." Minna leaned closer and pressed her lips to Kostroma's cheek. This time, she pulled back. "The black dragon will make it so, but his six eyes turn downward after-all. Lady Marzanna needs Simargł to ensure Prawia falls."

"They deserve eternal suffering, but…" Kostroma circled away with her fingers running along the chests of each guard she passed. Her attire was far less revealing than in the temple, but Minna still saw her beauty. As did the guards. They would have forgotten Lady Marzanna's promises out of lust, so their deaths and rebirths were necessary. Minna would need one to feed her *žityje* anyway. "I want to be the one who kills Strzybóg. It was his winds who blew my flower crown from my head, beginning the deception. Weles and Perun, among others, have wronged me too, but I shall settle for this one."

Minna smiled. "Acceptable."

"If this agreement is to be sustained, then I expect you to leave the rest of my guards alone until Marzanna holds up her end of the bargain," Kostroma continued, stopping before the guard beside the window. The man gave no reaction.

"This queendom means nothing to you. You will have your brother."

"And you shall become The Lady when I do. Until then, I rule. Understood?"

Minna approached her again, this time keeping a respectable distance just inside the moonlight from the window. "Fine, but I bow to only one."

Pride filled her as Kostroma nodded. She'd done it. Lady Marzanna had given her a final chance, and with Kupalo's appearance, Kostroma finally understood she needed an alliance to succeed. Surely, Minna would be rewarded. Each new life had been a gift from her goddess, but this was greater than any task she'd confronted before. Prawia would be theirs, and Minna would become queen of Solga.

Her, a queen.

"Your smile betrays you," Kostroma said after a moment of thought. "I thought you heartless like your mistress, but that is hope on your face. Get rid of it. Prawia holds beings more powerful than demons like me and even your goddess. Nothing from now on will be pretty." She raised a hand to Minna's cheek, claws now retracted. It was warm, almost inviting. "Keep the guards. Feed on them if necessary. You will need *žityje* to aid in the fight to come."

Then the miawka left her with the undead in the melilot mists. All else that remained was silence and a familiar chill that crept through the window. Minna clung to it, leaning over the sill and holding her cheek to the frigid glass. Finally, her time had come, and she swore to her goddess—and to herself—that she would not fail.

Not again.

8

Kostroma

KOSTROMA RETURNED TO EMPTY CHAMBERS for the first time in what seemed an eternity. Every night since she'd swayed Solga's leaders to name her queen, consorts and servants had greeted her in the wide room. Juliana and others would stand stiffly by the door, never stepping upon the fine blue rugs spread throughout the sitting area and around the plush bed, and consorts would drape themselves over chairs in their desperation for her attention.

Tonight, it was quiet. Darkness wrung away any warmth the room typically offered. The fireplace had died some time ago, and she'd demanded the windows be barred ever since her arrival. Sunlight affected even the most powerful of demons.

A single candle flickered atop the wooden table in the middle of the round-topped chairs. Roots wrapped around the table's leg and rim like a vine slowly choking its host. One stretched from each corner toward the candle, and when they met at the metal base—punched through with old tongue symbols that the craftsmen who made it had no understanding of—they twisted up the wax toward the flame.

Kostroma ran her fingers over the wall as she walked to one of the low dressers and pushed it open to reveal dozens of herbs and poisons in clouded glass vials.

Purple nightshade, burnet saxifrage, bits of birch bark, and more were all at her disposal for rituals and old spells she still tried to use at times. Though she was no longer the witch she'd been in life, *žityje* fueled demons the same as gods and mortals. She'd had a theory years ago that some of her godly channeling was still possible in spite of the demon's hunger constantly dwindling her life force, and she'd been right. No one knew she could still channel. For now.

She grabbed a jar of melilot, pouring it into her mortar before grinding it down and mixing it with the leaves with various other herbs. Her mother had taught her this combination as a child. Now, it was Kostroma's only way to speak with her.

It had been many years since she'd tried this ritual. Too long to forgive, but time passed to the gods far differently than it did for mortals. Unfortunately, those with gods' blood didn't forget like mortals did.

"Goddess of the night," Kostroma chanted in the old tongue as she brought the combined herbs to the candle, lighting them and allowing the smoke to spiral through the room until it grew so thick she inhaled nothing but it. "Goddess of swamps and waters, spirits and the drowned…"

She circled the table with her bowl in hand. The words hung in the air, power lingering in them like all words of the old tongue. Some called it the language of the gods, but she knew better. This was the language of power. The gods kept it to themselves and punished all mortals who used it without their permission, but it was not theirs to withhold.

"Answer me, Kupalnitsa," she pleaded. "Answer me, Mother. For I call to you in the night, in your domain. Demons wake beneath your veil, and of them, I am one. Take your servant. Take your daughter. Forgive my absence and allow me to hear your voice in my time of need."

The smoke filled her lungs more and more as she walked. Intoxicating, it drew her deeper into her mind, her soul. The room's chill fell away along with the soft falls of her feet against the rugs until her own thoughts consumed her. Deeper than those on the surface, they revealed the fears and desires she hid from even herself, but a sense of calm fell over her as the candle flickered out.

"A voice my ears have not been blessed with for a decade," Kupalnitsa's whisper said from within the room, constantly moving. "A voice that, yet, I have sought and heard, but never intended for me."

In the pure darkness, Kostroma couldn't see anything, but she felt the smoke shift around her as she continued to circle. It pressed upon her arms like an embrace. She tensed before responding, "I am sorry, Mother. My search for Kupalo has consumed me, and after our previous encounters… I… I worried you believed me to be a failure." She could deceive her servants and consorts, but the same could not be said of Kupalnitsa. Only the truth would do.

Kupalnitsa gave a heavy sigh. "Your folly centuries ago was taunting the gods. Perhaps, however, it was their folly to insight the rage of you and your father. I have heard your pact with Marzanna's szeptucha this night, and I know you well enough to predict that you have no intentions of completing your end of it."

"Then you know what I intend to do. The summer solstice…"

"My sisters will anticipate such action. Zorza Wieczorna and Zorza Poranna watch me closely each year as Simargł and I meet on the shortest night. You would know as such if you had not turned yourself into this ghastly form."

Of course. It never took Kupalnitsa long to remind Kostroma of her suicide. It's as if her mother believed she'd wanted to become a demon instead of remaining a goddess, finding love, and avoiding eternity as a blood devouring beast. "Don't pretend to care."

Kostroma had spoken before she'd thought about the words. Distance and feigned apathy had kept her from sparring with Kupalnitsa for centuries, but the truth remained the same, exposed by the herbs. The gods had betrayed her, yes. It was her mother that hadn't intervened to stop them.

"Centuries old," Kupalnitsa replied, "yet still foolish enough to believe I could have ended Perun and Strzybóg's games. Child, they would have killed me, trapping me as little more than nothing for an eternity until *žityje* mended my soul. What mother would not regret failing to stop her children's shared demise?" Her presence moved closer, tightening the mists' touch against Kostroma's skin. "I have never ceased loving you, Koska."

"Then help me!"

"I fail to see how I can change the inevitable end to your plan. With Marzanna's threat looming, my sisters will not be alone. Strzybóg has ignored his oath to protect Dziewanna on the equinox, but this time shall be different. He will be there…" The presence shifted, as if shuddering. "You will need more than a szeptucha and myself if you seek to face an elder god and the Zorza sisters."

Kostroma closed her eyes and breathed in deeply. Her thoughts slipped from her grasp until all she saw, all she heard, and all she smelled was the beast in the market alley. Blond and strong, all the presence of the godling she'd loved combined with the decay of the lowest upiór. She stared at him for a long time, questioning whether it had truly been him. What had he wanted? Why had he hidden for so long? The ritual revealed the truth, but she refused to believe it.

"Kupalo will be with us," she said. Each word stole the breath from her lungs, and she fought tears at the realization. He'd come to her, yet she'd run.

There was a pause before Kupalnitsa's reply. In that gap, Kostroma's heart ached with centuries of lingering anguish, loneliness. The gods had taken not only her brother and her life, but her entire family.

"You found him, then?" her mother asked. "Or did Marzanna catch him first?"

Kostroma winced. "The latter. I don't know how long she's entrapped him, but he came to me with her Frostmark carved into his back. He repeated her lies enough for me to fear it wasn't him, so I fled."

The ritual's whispers revealed otherwise. *"I couldn't face him. Not yet. Not like this… Like a beast."*

She hissed and spun away from her mother's presence, bumping into a chair and nearly sending the bowl of herbs flying. No matter how hard she tried, though, the voice—her voice—followed.

"I wasn't enough to face the gods then, alone. Why do I think I can now? Why would resisting bring anything but more pain?"

"Shut up!" she screamed aloud.

Kupalnitsa scoffed at her daughter's reaction, her words biting deeper than the whispers. "You are still a child. Admit your failures and mend what you are able to, like all other beings must. Unnatural death turned you to a miawka, but your soul was born that of a goddess. Act like it if you wish to retake the whole of your godly powers."

"How?" Kostroma turned to search for her mother in the darkness. "No demon has ever kept their godly soul."

"No god had ever fallen to corruption before you, yet you are not the last. Marzanna's actions clearly resemble the impulses of demonic hunger. Some could claim Jaryło's own do as well. They have long since Ascended, and their deific control over their forces remains in an altered form." A warmth met Kostroma's heart as Kupalnitsa's voice softened. "I see no reason that you could not regain control of the forces Rod chose you to wield. My insistence on your improvement is because of this fact: You remain my daughter and a goddess. Prove it."

The bowl slipped from Kostroma's hand, cracking against the floor. "How?"

"I know not how to mend your soul, but I am certain there is a path. Bring your brother, and begin where you fell. Understanding why you are what you are is the only way to become what you must be."

"I don't understand!" The vapor began to dissipate with the herbs no longer burning, and Kupalnitsa's presence faded. Chill replaced it. "Mother, tell me how."

A warmth touched her cheek. "Find me on the solstice with whoever you can bring and whatever piece of yourself you discover. Then we will know whether our vengeance shall come."

Then the warmth disappeared, and Kostroma dropped to her knees, her peasant clothes hanging to the floor. Her muscles shook. Her heart raced in her chest. With every moment, reality's sting grew, making her wish more for the sorcery's return, but she'd learned all she could. Kupalnitsa was right. The path forward was her own, and it was her responsibility to find it.

She pushed herself up. Mere days lay between this night and the solstice. Grief was a luxury she no longer had, so she rushed to the door, throwing it open and heading toward the throne room. With each step, she bit her cheek and pondered her next move. Marzanna had a plan. She had servants.

The Lady did too.

"Wake Commander Timo and Guard Captain Mikael," she told the first guard she saw in the entry hall. "Tell them our enemy doesn't rest, so neither shall we."

9

Kupalo

BLOOD FILLED THE BEAST'S SOUL. It coated his mouth, lingering upon his tongue until he knew of nothing else. The moon burned crimson, and all the twinkling souls in the night sky fell as he devoured them one-by-one.

"Forget her," Kupalo muttered to himself. "Forget…"

Heavy footfalls approached from either side of the wooden bridge he squatted on. His most recent meal—a balding, middle-aged man who'd worn a fine fur-lined coat—lay half-slumped over the side. As the guards shouted at him, he grabbed hold of each of the man's arms and spun, releasing the body toward one group.

The corpse hurled with inhuman force, its impact sending the first three shield-less guards tumbling into the undertrails below. Two remained on that side and three on the other.

Pitiful.

Kupalo charged the stunned pair on all fours. They swiped with short swords, but he was faster than a wolf and more powerful than a bear. At full speed, he dodged the first strike before grabbing the second's sword by the blade.

Black blood trickled from his hand. It mattered little. He'd gain more, growing larger and stronger with each victim's *żityje* he drained. The mere hours since he'd seen Kostroma had granted him an immense feeding that had doubled his bulk and satiated none of his hunger.

The guard tried fruitlessly to tear the sword free, but Kupalo yanked it away as the second guard swung. A decent strike, it would've killed a simple bandit. Mortal blades could do little to a fed upiór, though, and Kupalo blocked the thrust with ease. Then he drove the stolen blade through the guard's throat before his foe could even blink.

When he turned to the final guard on this side of the bridge, the man cowered, begging for mercy. Kupalo laughed.

"The Three Realms give no mercy."

He dug his fangs into the guard's neck with little resistance. Blood flowed into his maw like the finest nectar of the wilds, but he stopped before fully draining him. Death had scared the man. Let him cling to Jawia as the same beast he despised, then. Let him see what it was to be feared instead of enduring it.

Bells echoed through Rolika as Kupalo stood and stared across the bridge at the remaining guards. There were only two. He cursed. Of course, the third had run for aid when he'd seen what Kupalo was capable of.

More guards approached from every direction. He watched their shadows before glancing to the undertrails. Fleeing was the safest option, but something held him there for a moment longer. A tightening in his chest drew him toward the crowd on the opposing platform, where guards bowed their heads to a woman. She wore an immodest violet dress instead of the hooded coat from before, but he needed neither light nor familiar garb to recognize her.

Kostroma had come back.

He dropped his sword and slowly stepped onto the bridge. "So you've returned."

She mirrored the motion before stopping with her arms crossed. "Come, Brother. You have made quite the mess, and we have much to discuss."

"Then you have heard Marzanna's promise. You know what must happen?"

"I know what must happen." She furrowed her brow, then turned over her shoulder. "Follow, or there will be bloodshed—yours this time."

Kupalo ran his tongue over his fangs. The thought of continued combat tempted him, but he had a duty to his goddess. More than that, though, he needed to see Kostroma for real. He'd fled her gaze for so long, and now that she stood before him, he was unsure what to say.

He followed in silence.

Guards filtered in around them as they headed west, toward the palace. Thirty of them at least. Surely, it was overkill to bring so many to protect The Lady. They believed her to be a goddess after all, so what would thirty mortals do that she was incapable of? Kupalo grinned to himself. Mortals needed to feel important, and his sister understood that—no, *used* that. Marzanna had told him of Kostroma's imprudent use of her abilities as a miawka to seduce and drain men. Then again, hadn't Kupalo abused his own power as well? He felt no guilt, so why should she?

"What happened to you since we last spoke?" Kostroma asked as they rounded the edge of the market where he'd found her before. "You seem—"

"Upióry grow when we drain victims," Kupalo replied. His mind was slowly returning to some semblance of normal, the blood rage fading. "Fangs help with that."

"I've not seen many of your kind before. Miawki are more common now."

He raised his brows. "You should see Marzanna's Horde. There are hundreds of us now that she has Czarnobóg to mold mortal souls into the demons she desires."

The guards shifted uncomfortably around them. Kostroma laid a hand on her brother's arm, as his shoulder was a good three heads above her own now. "Let us speak more about this in private. Such things are not wise for mortals to hear."

Still, tension lingered among the guards all the way to the palace's entry hall, where two men in formal attire waited. The first held his hands behind his back and stood with a trained warrior's perfect posture. It was a rare sight among the tribes Kupalo had hidden with east of the mountain range the mortals called Perun's Crown, but the man's long brown hair was common among warriors in the north. Despite spending more time with the farmers and herders, Kupalo had learned enough about these kinds of men. He'd also learned what that longing gaze meant among mortal men.

"It seems this guardsman is fond of you," he whispered to his sister. "Charming."

She held her chin up without reply. "Commander Timo, thank you for rising so early and lending your aid in the search for my brother."

The man bowed his head. "My pleasure, Lady Kostroma. I hope this means I can recall my men from the search and focus our army on other pressing matters."

"We can discuss that in a moment. My brother and I must speak alone first."

"I beg your pardon?" the second man squawked. Stout with only a light dusting of gray across his sun-spotted head, his stomach seemed ready to burst out of his leathers. He held a wide stance, and his elbow pushed back a cape of violet trimmed in white as he touched the hilt of his blade. "This is a beast, surely not your god of a brother!"

A guard behind Kupalo chuckled, spurring him to spin and growl. "You find me funny?"

No reply came. He hadn't expected one, but the demonic whisper in his head urged him to prove a point. These mortals were to fear him, not mock him.

They have reason enough, he thought. *I never slaughtered large groups before Marz—*

The Frostmark flared upon Kupalo's back, sending him sprawling. Stone cracked beneath his fingers. Gathered guardsmen retreated with swords at the ready, and a few foolishly brave souls stepped between him and Kostroma. But he was no threat to her. No. Marzanna needed him, and he… he… he would serve.

The burning released at that stuttered acceptance. His demonic life before the winter goddess had been different, but as he rose, he reminded himself how she'd unleashed him. Marzanna had shown him what he could become. Soon, he'd have all his desires with Simargł's freedom—and his own.

"Kupek, what ails you?" Kostroma asked, helping him up with a worried glance at his mark. Obviously, she knew more than she admitted, but she'd always been better than him at understanding how to lie well. He would play along for her sake. "Do you want Guard Captain Mikael to be punished for his insults to your name?"

Kupalo waved a dismissive hand. "No. The opinions of a single guard mean nothing, no matter who he commands."

"You see, Mikael," Kostroma said with a grin back at the second man. "A monster would have killed you where you stand. Don't get me wrong, Kupalo is perfectly capable of doing so, but he is our ally. Understood?"

As Mikael searched for a reply, Kupalo took a small step toward him. Just enough for the guard captain to notice. "It would be a shame for us to start off on the wrong foot, as our goals are very much the same. Keep The Lady alive and ensure her interests are protected."

"Of course, Master Kupalo," Mikael grumbled. He stepped aside for them to pass, but his hand remained on his sword's pommel.

Had he not heard what had happened to his men who'd attacked Kupalo? A shame. The captain would be far angrier when he did, but that just made Kupalo gladder that he'd used his fangs carefully on the one guard, allowing him to become a upiór if not given his final rites. Mikael would see such a powerful demon as a gift if he were smart. Unfortunately, he appeared to hold the intellect of a toad.

Commander Timo twitched as Kostroma passed. His hand fell upon her arm, and he whispered far too softly for Kupalo to hear before allowing The Lady to continue on.

Has she finally found another lover after all these years? The rumors of her constant *usage* of consorts claimed otherwise.

Kupalo followed Kostroma down a passageway off the side of the entrance hall. He'd assumed at first that his twin would wish to speak formally in the throne room, but instead, she threw open the door to a smaller chamber. Chairs covered in cracked, worn leather filled half the room. A massive bed blanketed in furs and fine fabrics spanned the other.

Kostroma stood between the halves, her back to Kupalo. Her dress dipped low enough to reveal the skinless portions along her spine, and with her every movement, muscles contracted and expanded in harmony. Few mortals truly understood much about their bodies. They feared discovery beyond legends and accused healers of being witches. Why fear such immaculate forms? The fine workings of each tendon, vein, and bone wound together as a vessel for the soul—which the mortals were even further from grasping the true power of.

"They listen to you, worship you," he said once he'd shut the door. The chamber's rugs were soft against his bare feet, and though he knew it was warmer here than the snowfall outside, he felt no difference between them. A gift from Marzanna.

"They do," she replied, staring at a curtain-covered window. A few scattered candles offered light without the moon to creep through the glass beyond the fabric. "It meant nothing until I found you... Until you found me."

"You ran." A growl escaped his throat. Unintentional, it exposed an anger within him. He thought back to a time before that pull, but the searing of Marzanna's mark dampened those memories as he approached Kostroma. "My Frostmark frightens you."

She kept her back to him. "You hid from me. Where? I searched or centuries. I took this kingdom and sent scouts, armies! Then you come back as a shirtless beast of a man in a dark alley?"

"Mar—" Another flare of the Frostmark, but he pushed through its influence. "Marzanna is in my head. I was far to the east with a band of people who needed my help to survive, even if they did not know it. One upiór cannot face the Horde, however, and even as a god, I was never much of a fighter."

"I figured she'd imprisoned you. You had too much heart to bend to her will without torture."

Kupalo flinched, stumbling back as the Frostmark's pain deepened, locking his joints. All the agony of his imprisonment returned. Moons of ice colder than the deepest tundra slicing through his skin and bone as her whispers pierced his skull. If Marzanna was away, a szeptucha or other beast had replaced her, repeating the same phrases until they became his truth. All he knew. All he loved.

"My mistress is good," he mumbled when he regained his wits. "She showed me the truth, how to save Father. That's why she sent me to you."

He couldn't read Kostroma's expression in the dim light, but she glanced at him over her shoulder. "Why did you hide for so long? Mother couldn't even find you."

"I hated you for a time. You were the one who taunted the gods, and I was punished for it— twice. It was because of you that we followed

Sirin's call too. Each time, you left me alone, so I had no desire to see you again."

"You act like I wanted to leave you."

"Yet you did the moment we learned the truth." Kupalo puffed up his chest, closing his eyes and remembering their wedding ceremony. Unbraiding her hair. Taking her hand and gazing upon her smiling face. And their wedding night…

"She's your sister," the winds had laughed. *"The woman in your bed is the one who shared Kupalnitsa's womb with you."*

Kostroma crossed her arms and paced toward him. At the last moment, she turned sharply, throwing herself into a chair with her legs hung over one of the arms. She hadn't changed a bit.

"What did you expect me to do, hmm?" she asked. "Accept that I had bedded my brother because the gods decided to make a joke of me? Continue our marriage?" She pulled back her hair and lay her head to the side. Her eyes shimmered like gold in the candlelight as she watched him. "No, Kupek, I am not Marzanna. Her acceptance of familial relations led to her demise, and I couldn't allow myself to live on knowing I'd fallen for the same."

"All the Three Realms fear Marzanna now," Kupalo replied. "The gods suffer for supporting Jaryło over her. Why can you not be the same? Join her and you can be more than just the queen of a single tribe."

She grinned. "Good, she speaks to you infrequently."

He sat before her on the edge of the table. His fingers absently traced the roots around its rim— a winding knot waiting to be unbound. "I haven't an idea what you mean."

"I've formed a pact with her szeptucha in the other room. Minna, she calls herself, but there's something more there. She returned from death after I killed her, bearing a claim that you would be free from your Frostmark if I help release Father—if he serves her."

"Then why would she send me?"

"Because, dear brother," she said, taking his hand, "Marzanna knew I wouldn't accept Minna's offer without a push. Your appearance forced me to act. And act I have."

His chest tightened. "What have you done?"

Kostroma swept to her feet in a single motion. It was nearly morning, yet there was no weariness in her eyes, despite not feeding this night either. There was only the fierceness of a demoness. A goddess unbridled by fear. "I've set in motion the breaking of Father's cage. Simargł will be free, but I cannot tell you more because of the Frostmark you bear. So…"

She paused, pulling something from her bosom. Kupalo rose swiftly, but it was too late. A fine dust flew into the air with a swipe of her hand. "*Lędzi*," she whispered in the old tongue.

"No!" Kupalo snarled as his legs faltered. Whatever herbs she'd thrown clung to his face and entered his lungs with each weak breath. He collapsed into the nearest chair as his twin crouched before him, a single hand raised to his cheek.

"Sleep, Kupek," she breathed. "I will free us both when you wake."

10

Minna

"Do not trust her, my pet," Lady **Marzanna whispered** in Minna's mind. *"Remember who I have made you to be."*

The words of Minna's mistress lingered as she stood beside The Lady at the palace gates days after Kupalo's arrival. Warriors covered every bridge and platform in sight. A sea of iron and flesh, thousands of men had arrived from Solga's many villages as they planned to rescue Simargł on the solstice. One chance to free the fire god. One chance for Minna to prove her worth.

Commander Timo marched toward his men with his hands held behind his back. A tick of his, Minna had discovered in the past days of planning. It was a way to hide the severed finger on his sword-hand, but she wondered why he considered it a flaw. Minna wore her Frostmark scar with honor. Though his battle scar was different, it represented that he was a proud warrior, unlike the drunken generals who so often waited behind the lines in her old tribe.

My old tribe...

She sucked in a sharp breath as the commander began his speech to rally the men. Images flashed before her: a small village of wooden houses partially sunken into the earth, a family surrounding her and shouting to Prawia that she would be Perun's chosen, and a hunchbacked girl who looked at her like a wounded dog. *Radojka...*

The visions felt so *real.* She could smell the stew prepared by a woman who bore a stark resemblance to her. *Mother?* No, it couldn't be. Her mother had died in childbirth, and the Lady Marzanna had taken her in, raised her to become a szeptucha. Then why couldn't she remember any of her childhood beyond these strange visions? No matter how hard she fought them, more came, pushing deeper until her head ached and she swayed on her feet. Then came the worst of all.

A dense swamp surrounded her and Radojka, its mud caking her boots up to the ankle as she sloshed after a graying man dressed in robes embroidered in red. That was significant... How? A swarm of thoughts pounded Minna's head, but those she needed stretched out of reach. The memory went on regardless, heading deeper into the swamp until stopping suddenly before a large pond.

The man turned to Minna. She recognized his face beneath the Forgemark of Swaróg on his leather headband. A name came with it—Dariusz. Just there in her mind, as if a door had been latched shut, and all she'd needed to do to open it was push hard enough. Always there... hidden.

Then she drowned, pressed down into the bed of the pond by the man—the priest, she remembered. Dariusz was elderly, but he knew his purpose as she tried to fight free. What? Why was she drowning? Why had she caught sight of the hunchback girl's face out of the corner of her eye?

"Save me, Perun!" her voice screamed in her head. *"Anyone!"*

No savior arrived. Minna writhed and fought, but water surged down her throat until it pushed away the air from her lungs. What hope she'd possessed faded, leaving only the dread of death.

Her first. Darkness overtook her for longer than she could know.

Then a voice called, tearing her from a torturous sleep.

"Perun has denied you," the winter goddess sang. "The rest have forgotten you. So I will make you mine. I will slay Death for his betrayal and drag you from the earth, for you are more than a szeptucha, Vida. You are to become my muse, and with your death, I will conquer the living realm."

A hand fell upon Minna's shoulder, tearing her brutally back to reality as she stumbled back, gasping. "Who is Vida?"

"I have seen that look more times than I can count," Kostroma whispered with a knowing grin. "What visions did your lady show you this time? Help to kill three gods, I hope."

"No, I…" Minna fought to regain her wits. She was supposed to be an intimidating presence to Kostroma, to show her Lady Marzanna's power, but the vision had her drowning—again. "I saw visions of a past. It was both mine and not."

Kostroma narrowed her eyes before returning to a more queenlike posture. "Listen to them. We lose ourselves when we ignore the difficult thoughts."

A cheer echoed through Rolika's bridges as Commander Timo finished his speech with a raised fist. Minna had heard none of it, but from the warriors' reactions, it had done the job. Both she and Kostroma knew facing the Zorza sisters and Strzybóg would be impossible for mortals. Luckily, their deaths were part of her lady's plan.

"The solstice is in two days," Minna said. "Lady Marzanna has granted you Kupalo as promised. Do your part, and you'll both be free."

Kostroma held her chin high. "I remember our agreement."

"Yet you exclude me from your meetings to plan the assault itself."

"You know what you must. Kupalo and I will face the gods as my army provides much needed distractions for whatever allies they'll have near. Where and how my mother and father meet on the solstice is my business alone."

Minna sneered down at her. "Do you want Lady Marzanna's help or not? She is the frozen queen! Jawia is hers, yet you question the true goddess—"

"Do not speak to me of goddesses and queens!" Kostroma demanded, silencing the gathered warriors. Commander Timo turned back to the pair, but Kostroma's glare was fixed upon Minna. Death swirled in her gaze. It reminded Minna of her mistress, but there was something else there that was missing in Lady Marzanna. A passion.

"Your goddess can speak to me herself if she is so desperate to know where we'll strike," Kostroma continued. "You may be her pet, but I am not."

Frost spread around Minna's feet as ice formed at her fingertips. "She is giving you everything you wanted," she whispered in the rhythm of a chant. "Your brother. Your lover. Your father. All she asks is Simargł's aid in exacting the revenge both she and your family so desperately need. Why do you fear your desires?"

Guards closed in around them, their shuffled steps revealing their advance, but Minna kept her gaze upon Kostroma. Fools. All she'd need to do was command the frost to snatch their ankles. It had grown over an area at least fifteen strides in each direction, and the *žityje* would've been worth it if Marzanna hadn't commanded her to act carefully. Why? Caution was for the weak. As the stronger force, the Frostmarked needed to strike, not wait for a demon's aid.

But Minna stepped away. The ice dissipated from her hands as she held them out at her sides. "The true queen's embrace is ready when you choose to accept it."

Then she turned with a sweep of her long cloak, leaving Kostroma and the army in silence. Only one brave guard tried to stop her, but Kostroma's voice cut through the wind when he grabbed Minna's arm.

"Leave her," Kostroma said. "We will need her and her lady in the days ahead. There are far more fearsome powers in the Three Realms than a szeptucha who's too afraid to die."

11

Kostroma

"WE MARCH THEM TO THEIR DEATHS."

Hands held behind him, the ever-positive Commander Timo paced at the base of the steps before Kostroma's throne. She would've scorned most for the distracting motion, but Timo was adorable when he was flustered. Warriors hid their anxieties more than anyone. That made it all the more refreshing to know he trusted her enough to reveal that side of himself.

Kostroma took in a deep sigh, crossing her legs. Her embroidered dress's mountains of indigo fabric covered her enough to almost block sight of Timo below. Solgawi beauty standards were a bore. She yearned to return to her temple and free her skin, but she'd waited too long for her brother's return. He lay unconscious in her chambers for the time being. Once he woke, she needed to be ready to counter Marzanna's plans with her own. Pleasure could wait.

"Tell me what I should do, then," she said. "These are your men. You know how they think, how they fight."

He stopped to the side. His stump of a finger wiggled at his back as he thought, staring at the ground. It was just the two of them in the throne room, and that alone was against decorum enough to drive a stickler like Timo insane. "My apologies, Lady Kostroma, but they fear what you ask of them. We intend to face three deities and deceive another. My men are determined, loyal. This…" He looked at her over his shoulder, worry evident in his eyes. "This is enough to make the bravest warrior quake in his boots."

"Yet you do not," she offered with a playful laugh. "Fear is natural, but you do not quiver or flee."

He straightened his posture and turned to her. An officer's stance, not an advisor's or friend's. It was hard for Kostroma to know what he was to her, but the formality made her chest ache. "I am loyal to you, my lady. You have my trust and my sword no matter what we face, but my men do not know you as I do. Skepticism breeds discontent. Discontent leads to desertion and chaos. We can afford neither during the war ahead."

"Not ahead."

"I'm sorry, my lady, but I don't understand."

Slowly, she rose, descending the throne's steps with her skirts following her as if she were the tide and they the rushing waters. Timo held his ground, but swallowed when she stopped before him—too close for a queen and commander. Still, he did not retreat. Good.

"The war is not ahead," she said. The echo amplified her voice here, and she took a moment to revel in the reminder of the power she wielded. "It began the moment Minna entered my temple… No, the moment she stepped foot in Rolika. Men think of wars as battles and blood, but the most dangerous ones begin quietly. Kings fall because they fail to realize it is the games in the shadows that determine the winner on the battlefield far before the first sword is drawn from its sheath."

"Flanking the enemy and bringing superior numbers is one thing," Timo replied. "Defeating deities is another."

She grinned. "Then it is good that neither they nor Marzanna know what I do." Kostroma's mother had not provided answers, but the thought of returning to where everything fell apart had given her an idea. One that could prevent her people's slaughter. *When did I start caring about their lives?*

"And that is?"

"I trust you, Timo," she whispered, "but the gods' ears are everywhere. They have known who I am for many years. Anyone and anything in this palace could serve them. Though our plan remains, know that I have no intention of forcing your men to fall to any deity's power. Remember the threat in the east remains and understand that your warriors must remain vigilant, even in victory. Freeing Simargł will not be the end."

With a short step back, Timo bowed. "Very well, my lady. And what of Kupalo? There are… concerns… that he has not been seen since his arrival."

"Of course they noticed." Kostroma grimaced and turned toward one of the windows. The sunlight streaming through it gave warmth to mortals, but it made her demonic soul want to shrivel into dust. Too often, she overestimated mortal ignorance. Kupalo was an upiór now.

Bringing him into the palace inevitably drew attention, and the whispers would only spread. "The Frostmark upon his back makes him too exposed to Marzanna. I need him sedated until we are ready."

"Minna will warn her goddess if he's gone any longer."

She looked back at him. "Then what do you suggest?"

The commander stiffened, straightening the straps holding his cape in place. Any casualness that had slipped into his voice disappeared. "I do not know enough to foresee your plan, but I believe you should keep him close. Ensure he trusts you. We have spent years searching for him, only for him to fall at our feet. Whatever part he has to play, it is better for him to remain our ally, Frostmarked or not. Sedation acts against this."

"Thank you for your candor." Kostroma raised her arm toward the door. "Now go and prepare. We march at dawn tomorrow."

"I suppose this means you still won't tell me where to."

"We will meet where the Sirin calls along the riverbank, where this all started."

A part of her itched to tell him more, but she made for the throne room doors herself. There was too much at risk. After centuries of suffering, she'd finally have her family and life back as long as Kupalo could defy Marzanna for even a moment. One heartbeat. That's all she needed. But if she was going to get even that, Timo was right.

She needed to wake Kupalo, no matter the pain that followed.

12

Kupalo

KUPALO FLOATED THROUGH THE CLOUDS, drifting ever upward through the masses of white and gray. They were cool upon his skin. Not the chill of Marzanna's ice but the gentle touch of a bath in an autumn stream. He welcomed their embrace until the clouds turned to wisps and then nothing.

Mortals wondered often about what lay beyond the clouds. Krowikie and Astiwie, whatever remained of them, claimed it was the realm of the gods, untouchable by man and demon alike. Kupalo's old friend among the eastern tribes thought instead that there was nothing above. To them, the sun was the tip of the sun god's flaming arrow. Every tribe had a different name for Dadźbóg, but they all worship him nonetheless for his light and heat.

There was no sun here.

Light pierced this realm regardless. Ever-present, it banished all shadows and revealed stacked rings of hundreds of floating landmasses, threaded between by winding wooden paths that connected each to a massive tower in the rings' centers—like branches stretching from a tree trunk. Kupalo could not tell much about the islands from below, but roots stuck through their earth, which resembled the shape of an acorn. Grasses and vines hung over the edges in places too. Though a precarious position for plants, he'd learned over the centuries how hardy many could be.

A fog drifted through Kupalo's mind, despite the clear air. Sounds were dampened, and the floating islands appeared impossibly far. He tried to raise his arm and reach for them. It was futile. The shoulder wouldn't even budge, so he let his limbs hang as he rose beyond the lowest islands.

Blurred, confusing images filled his mind during the journey. Kostroma was in each, but she looked at him as if he were a stranger… no, a monster. Why? And what was that frigid sensation creeping down his spine each time he saw her? She'd finally found him. Shouldn't she be ha—

How did I escape?

The thought hit him so suddenly that it knocked the air from his lungs. Escape from where? He'd been avoiding his past in his east, and then visitors showed up. Undead riders wielding bone weapons and threatening his new tribe. He remembered the battle that followed, the hundreds of Horde riders he'd slain, and the screams of his allies. A man upon a white horse had approached him, promising to spare the others if Kupalo came with him, so he'd gone.

"Koschei," his voice called into the vast realm before him. With his mind fighting his awakened senses, it sounded alien, dead. "The deathless sorcerer. I remember… He took me to Marzanna."

Pain shot across his back. The fog dulled none of it, and he cried out as his muscles spasmed and his limbs flailed against his control. The chill grew from a trickle to a flood. Whispers came with it, commands that he dared not resist. Why would he? The pain was sharp, but when he listened, there was only the sweet voice. His goddess's voice.

"No!" he shouted through gritted teeth. "You'll betray her! You'll destroy everything!"

"Hush my pet," Marzanna hissed in his head. *"Remember that it is I who freed you and awakened the beast. You are strong because I will it, because I need you."*

Kupalo coughed, his throat refusing to let him speak until he pushed through the resistance. "You need Simargł. You'll… You'll use him."

"I'll give him what he wants. Nothing less."

An island loomed before him now. Unlike many of the others, it was lifeless. Dirt and ash spiraled across its flat surface with the wind, and as he stepped upon it, an empty feeling took hold of his chest.

A female figure took form beside him, made of the inconstant ash. "This was once your father's home. Do you know what happened to it?"

Kupalo clenched his fists. Now in full control of his senses, he let his anger grow as he stared over what should have become his palace in Prawia. "The gods destroyed it. They stole it from Father, from us!"

"Yes, and I shall return it to you so long as you aid me. Do not listen to Kostroma's lies. She seeks to unravel all that we have planned. We need her to defeat the Zorza sisters and release

Simargł's binds, but that is it." She stepped closer, her voice turning harsh. "Your toils have been because of her folly. End her and be free to become the mighty god you were meant to be."

"I will rid the Three Realms of her when the time comes," he replied. No thought had gone into the words, but he knew them to be true. Why would the Lady Marzanna seek to deceive him?

The winds began to tear at her form, each speck of ash flying into the endless sky. "I am glad to hear it, as she is calling you back now. Remember my commands, Kupalo. I will be waiting."

Then the goddess disappeared with the last of the ash. Kupalo watched her go before walking toward the center of the massive island. Larger than a small city, it could have easily held a god's palace, and black scars across the ground revealed where walls had crumbled, likely against the might of Perun's lightning and Swaróg's celestial fire. Simargł had revolted against their manipulation of his children, so they destroyed his palace and imprisoned him forever.

"Perun, god of justice." Kupalo scoffed. "You'll taste justice by the flame."

A force pulled him back. He slid, and though he tried to dig his boots into the ground's ruts, the force was stronger. The entire island seemed to turn on end. Soon, he reached the edge, and with one last look at the realm that should have been his home, he fell back to the mortal realm.

***

Cold. Dark. Kupalo shivered and stared up at the ceiling of Kostroma's chambers, the flickering candlelight casting upon it a shadow of the figure before him.

"You used witchcraft on me," he mumbled. His tongue was dry and felt larger than it should've. He licked his lips to regain some sensation, but only succeeded at cutting himself on his fangs.

Kostroma crouched, her mouth curled in a wry smile. It was unfair that she was his twin. She'd pleasured herself with most of Rolika it seemed, but he could never forget how he'd loved her. All of it had been a lie crafted by the gods. Still… She was a beautiful woman.

"I did," she said sternly, "and I don't regret it. You bear a Frostmark."

He rubbed his head. It ached too as he shook off the effects of Kostroma's spell. "What are you hiding? Ack. How long has it even been?"

"The solstice is tomorrow."

"Kostka!" He raged, throwing himself out of the chair and shooting to the door. "You can't save Father without me, yet you entrance me with your magic as you plan the assault? Imbecile."

Her face was a blank slate as she paced toward him. "The Kupalo I knew would never hold such anger. You were a god of peace. How do you know I need you to free him?"

"You would've done it already otherwise," he replied, averting his gaze.

Now her brow furrowed. Yes, it had been Marzanna who'd told him that he was needed for the rescue, but Kostroma had no proof to deny his logic. What his help entailed, however, even Marzanna didn't know. He would have to follow Kostroma until she revealed the truth. Only then could he fulfill his vow to the goddess.

"You're right," Kostroma admitted, arms crossed. "I need you. In truth, I always have, but you ran from me." Despite her sharpened tone, she stepped closer. "You are here now, though, and I'm realizing that's what matters. I still love you as my brother. That will never change."

Kupalo's stomach twisted into a knot, but the cold press upon his mind urged him to focus. He had a role to play. "Then bring me into your planning. Tell me what I must do to reunite our family."

"I would rather show you."

She thrust out her arms. Smoke followed, billowing through the space between them as she whispered in the old tongue again. Visions pulled at Kupalo's mind, and he slipped from reality before he had the chance to resist.

When he blinked, he stood at a forested riverbend beneath a dark sky full of twinkling souls. Singing filled the air. Sweet, enticing, it was enough to pull at any man's heartstrings, but Kupalo's blood chilled at the sound. The song haunted him each night—Sirin's voice. Hers was the last voice he'd heard in Jawia for many years. The gods had sent her for a reason.

Another song echoed not far away, where a young girl danced with a creature whose legs and body were that of a radiant bird and whose head was a stunning woman. Colors streamed from Alkonost's extended wings, and little Kostroma gawked as she danced to the tune. She knew nothing of her brother in those moments. It was only her and Alkonost, caught in bliss as Sirin dragged Kupalo away to Weles's realm.

The cries of his younger self pulled Kupalo closer to the river. His dread grew heavier with each step, but he needed to see it again. No matter how much the agony in his heart cried for him to stop, he plodded on through the forest until Sirin appeared.

He bared his fangs and hissed, but Sirin did not yield to his grown form. She sang on with her beauty and bird-like body resembling those of Alkonost. No bright colors flowed from her wings, though. Instead, there was darkness, and as young Kupalo drew closer with his blue eyes wide and blond hair drifting through the gales, it grabbed hold of his ankles.

"Fight it," Kupalo whispered to himself through tears. "You can still live…"

The boy gave no resistance as Sirin led him toward the bank of the wide Avka River. Legends told that every river led to Weles's realm in Nawia. Kupalo had never believed them as a child, but he'd been so very wrong. Unlike the priests' claims of paradise in the afterlife, the Way of Souls was unforgiving, forcing the dead to endure much before reaching anything close to those tales. Kupalo had been only a boy. He'd not been ready. If only the gods had cared what he wanted.

Kupalo dropped to his knees, watching his younger self disappear beneath the waters, not to return for many years. He cursed the gods. He cursed Kostroma for leaving him to Sirin. He cursed himself for being too weak to resist.

Night became day in moments. Kupalo raised his head as the sun beat upon him, drawing sweat from his brow as the river stirred.

A young man rose from the exact place where the boy had disappeared. Kupalo knew his own face well, and little had changed since this moment, beyond the demon's effects. He was no longer a child. Fit as a workhorse, he'd Ascended and served Weles well to earn his release.

Little had he known then that Weles had only let him go as part of a greater plot against Simargł. Kupalo's father had created more and more problems for Swaróg and his two most favored sons. Perun and Weles rarely ended their quarrels, but to defeat their hated uncle at Swaróg's behest, they would do anything, including using children as part of their game.

Taking Kupalo from Jawia had been Weles's trick. Now, Perun's arrived in the form of a flower crown floating down the river. He and Strzybóg had used wind and storm to send Kostroma's wreath away, but young Kupalo hadn't known. He'd thought himself lucky that he'd found a maiden to wed so quickly.

Kupalo turned away as the young man picked the wreath from the Avka's flow. So many mistakes, all caused by the gods.

When the scene shifted again, he stood within a sea of purple and blue flowering plants. They covered the riverbed where Sirin had taken him and where he'd returned. Kupalo-da-Miawka flowers—the gods' pitiful attempt at apologizing for ruining Kupalo and his twin's lives. No flower could mend what they had broken, but this was why Kostroma had shown him this. It was where the gods had deceived. Perhaps, it was also where they could exact their revenge.

He took one of the flowers and studied its two colors. Indigo for Kostroma. Yellow for him. Mortals thought of yellow as a joyous color, attaching it to the sun, but Kupalo felt no joy. He hadn't for a long time.

The vision faded around him, and in those last breaths, he held the flower into the sunlight. Then he crushed it.

13

Minna

MINNA ROUNDED THE PILLARS IN THE PALACE'S ENTRANCE HALL for what seemed the hundredth time, driving her boots hard into the stone with each step. How dare Kostroma make her wait. It was the day of the summer solstice, a day opposed to her goddess on the typical year, but Lady Marzanna's blizzards ruled the warmest moons now. Even she couldn't extend the window of opportunity to free Simargł, though. They needed to act before the next morning or lose the chance for another year.

Lady Marzanna would never forgive her then.

"You, guard," Minna barked *again* at the nearest guardsman beside the throne room door. A brazier by his side reflected brilliantly off his chain mail armor, but his strong appearance faltered as he visibly quivered at her continued questioning. "Tell The Lady to see me, or I'll knock down this door myself."

"I… I told you before, Lady Minna, that—"

Ice daggers fell into her grasp as she charged, pinning him to the wall with one blade to his throat. "You were saying?"

At that, the door swung open. Commander Timo emerged alongside Kupalo, and the latter gave Minna a nod when he noticed her. Good. Lady Marzanna's plan was still in motion. Minna's goddess had all but pushed her aside since Kupalo's arrival, but she would prove herself worthy of becoming the Lady of Rolika.

Kostroma appeared not far behind. She raised her brow at Minna and the blade to her guard's throat. "You will find finer sacrifices to Marzanna among our enemies. Come. We march west."

"I must inform Lady Marzanna," Minna said, withdrawing from the guard but keeping her blades in hand.

"She already knows," Kupalo replied.

Minna gritted her teeth at yet another rejection from her goddess. She'd always served to the best of her ability. Why had Lady Marzanna forsaken her for an upiór who was too blinded by his affection for Kostroma to finish her off? He listened to commands now, but Minna doubted he could actually kill the woman he loved.

Don't expose your anger, she told herself. *You will be The Lady. Soon...*

So she followed the others into the city. With the winds coming from the east, Rolika's stench of refuse and smoke met them beyond the palace. It was a disgusting place that Minna promised herself she'd fix. Lady Marzanna would rule the Three Realms, and Minna would reign as one queen among her lands. A new world for her to shape.

Commander Timo and around fifty guards escorted the group over the bridges, toward the massive wall along Rolika's western edge. Near complete now, it was far larger than Huebia's walls. Minna couldn't help but stare in awe at the sheer amount of stone separating the city from the wilds beyond. A wall couldn't keep out the Frostmarked Horde, though. Nor could it protect the east when Lady Marzanna chose to crush Kostroma's fertility magic, freezing the Avka River and the forests that had resisted winter's control for now. Kostroma had some plan to deceive Minna. That much Minna was sure of. But plans were irrelevant against the power of Lady Marzanna.

Minna's awe shifted to discomfort as they neared the gate passing through the wall. Barebacked slaves hauled stone after stone through the dug alleyways below. Blood stained sections of the wall a deep crimson, and their exposed skin was sliced and beaten in many places, likely from whips and cudgels. They had built the wall quickly. At what cost?

Why do I scorn Kostroma for acting as I did in Huebia? she asked herself. *There are those meant to lead, those meant to follow, and those too disloyal to be allowed to live.* Lady Marzanna made use of the disloyal before demanding their sacrifice. Was it all that different for Kostroma to do the same?

Of course it wasn't the same. Kostroma's offerings and control were built on the lies of a false goddess. Any sacrifice for Lady Marzanna was worth it because she was the rightful ruler, and she would not use deceit against her own people.

The army met them on the path beyond. They stood in rows in cleared sections of the forest. Beyond, trees fought, keeping their leaves with Kostroma's power feeding them, but she was only a miawka. She hadn't fed in days based on the rumors of the servants. Even now, she was weaker than when she'd defeated Minna in her temple. Minna could see it in the rings under her eyes and the shortness of her breath. Demonic hunger would take her, and that would make it all the easier to kill her when the time came.

Other heavily armored men approached Commander Timo as Minna mounted her horse, following Kostroma and Kupalo's leads. It was small. She'd likely been given the stubborn beast as extra hinderance to prevent her acting apart from Kostroma's plan. She smirked at that. Kostroma had thought of everything, but it wouldn't be enough.

"Is everything prepared for the march?" Kostroma asked Timo when he was finished.

He held a fist to his chest and bowed slightly, a formality Minna hadn't seen him do within the palace. "We are ready, my lady. As long as we don't encounter any resistance, we should reach the grove by nightfall."

She signaled for him to mount. "Then we march."

From there on, no one passed Kostroma. Only she—and apparently Kupalo—knew the true location of the meeting place between Kupalnitsa and Simargł. It fascinated Minna that so many gods could meet without anyone else discovering the location.

Not gods, her voice snapped at her. *Deceivers. Fiends.*

That anger pulled her in, stealing her thoughts for a long while, but she didn't mind. Instead, that rage felt natural. She was meant to fight and serve her goddess, not to wonder about deities. A wandering mind was a distraction.

Dadźbóg's sun seemed to sprint toward the horizon. Another god who'd sided with Jaryło against Lady Marzanna. Her growing power had weakened his warmth, and Minna grinned at the continued chill that gripped the air, enough for her to blow out fog before her. Each step brought her closer to her crown.

"The lands shall fall," she whispered. "The rivers shall freeze. Walls will crumble before her might."

Dusk approached by the time the Kupalo-da-Miawka flowers appeared. While the other flora barely clung to life, these thrived in brilliant blue and bright yellow. There were few at first, but they quickly covered the forest, spreading toward the Avka River to their right. The flower was unlike any Minna had seen before. A shame its namesake would have to die—again.

Darkness came soon after, and its quiet took Minna by surprise. She'd been so entranced by the flowers and consumed by Lady Marzanna's commands that she hadn't noticed the lack of footfalls behind her. Her chest tightened, and as she looked over her shoulder, she cursed Jaryło.

The army was gone.

"What is this?" she called ahead to Kostroma. "Where are your allies?"

No reply came, and even Kupalo glanced at his sister with doubt. Was there finally something she'd hidden from him too?

"You promised Lady Marzanna that you would bring the full force of your power," Minna continued. "Yet you leave us to face three false gods with only us and my lady!"

This time, Kostroma gave a huff. "I did not lie." Then she turned sharply toward the river, snatching Kupalo's arm and tearing him free from his horse before he could do anything but yelp.

Everything went black. Frost chilled Minna's veins, and when her vision returned, she was charging toward the river, ice shooting from her hands. Dozens of bolts were already embedded in the trees ahead. Kostroma's horse bleed profusely from its side, but still, she dragged her brother on as he slashed at her now shredded arm.

There was no time to think, but fear clutched Minna at the blackout. Why didn't she remember attacking? What was Kostroma doing? Had this happened before?

She had no answers. Attacking was her only option, but Kostroma was already half submerged in the wide river. She'd ripped her riding dress, exposing her skinless miawka back and claws that clutched Kupalo as he tried to fight free. The Lady had seemed a queen at times. Now, she was nothing but a demon dragging away Minna's only ally.

But the ice bolts were no use. Despite half-a-dozen sticking out of Kostroma's torso, she screamed and pulled Kupalo beneath the surface. Both her and her horse's blood turned the river a swirling crimson-black. Minna was too late.

So she called her goddess.

Throwing herself to the ground, Minna summoned an ice dagger. She held its tip to her palm and looked to the sky as she chanted in the old tongue, "Take my blood, mother of the dead. Come to me, patron of the outcast. Fulfill your wrath, queen of the frost."

Power burst through her as she slit her hand wrist to finger. The air shimmered with the glowing Frostmark upon her eye, burning like snow against an open wound. Her goddess was coming. Her lady would have her victory.

Footsteps approached from behind, but Minna kept her focus on the light of her Frostmark. A form began to take shape in it as snow fell from the gathering clouds. This was the solstice, the night where the Three Realms were closer than ever and magic was at its greatest. She felt all of it.

"Vida," a rough, scratchy voice said as the footsteps stopped and a hand fell upon Minna's shoulder. "Vida, I'm sorry." Minna froze at that name. The same one from her visions. It echoed through her mind as the voice whispered in her ear, "*Sěti.*"

Remember.

Visions raced before her faster than she could comprehend. They all showed the hunchbacked girl, staring at her with her cleft lip distorting her smile. Minna clung to the images and pushed in hopes of remembering something about her. These were memories, likely ones that had been lost in her many deaths, but maybe Lady

Marzanna was showing her them slowly. Maybe her goddess hadn't forgotten her.

"Radojka," Minna giggled in the memory as her younger self stood with a group of girls across the field from the hunchback. "It's good she stares at her feet, so no one has to see her face."

That mocking laughter echoed through each memory of the girl until they walked together with the priest Minna recalled as Dariusz. The one who'd drowned her.

Radojka clutched Minna's hand, staring up at her with hope. "Perun will choose you," she said. "Maybe he'll choose us both."

"He only chooses the best," young Minna replied. *And that's certainly not you.*

Another black-haired girl walked with them. She held a Bowmark amulet of the spring goddess Dziewanna, clutching it so tightly that it had to hurt. An image flashed before Minna. It showed the same girl standing before her as Minna plunged a dagger into her own head. Why?

The memory flashed forward, beyond the ritual in the swamp. Beyond the living realm.

Minna knelt in the black sand she'd felt too many times. Instead of awe and the glory of her lady's presence, though, all she felt was pain. Blood streamed down her arms and torso. It covered her eyes so thick she struggled to see and her nose enough to make each breath a nightmare. She became aware of the horrible feeling across the left side of her face. What sight she had was shifted, and as she crawled toward the burning Smorodina river, she dreaded what she would see. She knew. She'd always known, as she bore that scar to this day. The mark of her savior, her goddess.

Her captor.

Screams echoed through the memory as she saw her reflection. Gouges crossed over her left eye in jagged slashes, surely from Lady Marzanna's claws.

"These are gifts," the goddess claimed from behind her as a force grabbed her leg. "For every piece I take from you, the more I give in return."

Minna trembled, trying to pull herself into the current, into Nawia. "Let me die!"

"Oh, my pet." The goddess pulled Minna to her and pushed up her chin. The motion forced her to take in the winter goddess's presence, and Minna saw not beauty but horror. "That is the one thing I cannot do."

An onslaught of memories followed. One after another, they recounted torture and sorcery wiping Minna's mind and replacing her thoughts with Lady Marzanna's whispers… No. This beast scraping her, devouring her, was no lady. And she was not Minna.

She sucked in a sharp breath at reality's return, falling back into the embrace of the woman behind her.

"Radojka," she whispered, the name pulsing so strongly it pushed away all the memories of pain. "My sister. My twin…"

"Yes, Vidka," the woman replied, smiling down at her with the same distorted smile as in Minna's… *Vida's*… memories. Except this time, Vida saw the gentle kindness in it. "Weles sent me to remind you who you are, so I can take you from this place."

Words escaped Vida. She trembled at the memories, but she knew their truth in her soul. This was who she truly was. Not Marzanna's pet but Vida, a girl so desperate to be chosen that she'd clung to Marzanna when the gods rejected her.

"I can't leave," she mumbled.

Radojka shook her head. "You must. Kostroma will kill you for what you've done."

"No." A strange feeling told Vida that wasn't true. Despite her scorn for Marzanna, Kostroma had allowed Vida to feast upon her guards for *žityje* and had shown her an odd sense of care. They were both fallen, broken. Could Kostroma mend her soul if she survived? "I have to help her."

"You can choose. That's all I wanted."

Radojka's touch disappeared as a series of cracking noises came from the river. Vida scrambled for her sister, but she was gone. *I'll find you again,* she promised herself. *I'll fix this.*

When she turned back to the river, ice spread from the far bank as Kostroma and Kupalo burst from the shallows together. It stretched toward the pair like tendrils, but they scampered onto the shore—right into the swirling mist of snow Vida had called moments before.

The mists took form as the twins collapsed at the figure's feet. Long black hair fell over the woman's shoulders as the snow formed her dress of white, lined with black symbols of the old tongue. Vida's entire body froze at the sight of her goddess. Lady Marzanna had come, and Vida realized in that moment why she'd killed herself to forget in Huebia.

Knowing the true monster she served was more painful than death.

14

Kostroma

"I'M SORRY, KUPEK."

Beneath the Avka's surface, Kostroma felt life for the first time in centuries despite the ice bolts piercing her body. It was here that she'd lost Kupalo. It was here that he'd returned. It was here that she'd become a miawka. And it was here that she was reborn.

"I forgive you for leaving," she spoke through the water, "for running. You are my brother, and I will always love you as one."

Kupalo had struggled against her pull, but now, he held tight to her as *žityje* rushed through her, healing her wounds. The demonic hunger that had become deafening in recent days vanished. She hoped the ritual did the same for him, as an ending to both their suffering apart. A cycle complete. A connection reborn.

A blizzard met them when they burst from the water. Kostroma still possessed her miawka claws, speed, and skinless back, but the change within her signaled it had worked. One couldn't undo their corruption into a demon. She'd had no intention of doing that. All she wanted was to restore what she'd lost, and that started with making right her relationship with Kupalo.

It ended with killing the gods.

Ice shot across the river and snatched at Kostroma's ankles, but she pulled herself free, tumbling into the Kupalo-da-Miawka flowers with Kupalo at her side. Minna's ice bolts had ripped parts of his tunic. Just a few cuts—enough to reveal the lack of a Frostmark on his back. A goddess could mark anyone, but he'd regained his godly soul through the mending of their bond, burning away her influence.

Someone stood over them. Kostroma realized it too late, and when she moved to strike, her feet refused to budge, frozen to the earth.

"You are quite a surprise, Kostroma." A deathly pale woman dressed in a flowing dress of white smirked down at her. Black Frostmarks joined Czarnobóg's Darkmark along her sleeves and hem, but Kostroma didn't need any hint to know she faced Marzanna in the flesh. "Unfortunately, you are far less surprising than you believe."

Kostroma gritted her teeth and reached for the pool of *žityje* that had reentered her soul. No longer consumed by the demon, it could now fuel her godly powers—water and fertility. "His Frostmark is gone, Marzanna. My brother is mine, and so too will my father."

"We shall see, but before anything can change, you must release Simargł." Marzanna gave a knowing grin. "Did your ritual work as you intended?"

"You knew?"

Kupalo groaned, pushing himself to his knees. "Knew what?"

Marzanna offered him her hand. "Demonic corruption can be partially mended by finding its source and either defeating or fixing the *unnatural* aspect. I have known this for many years. Both your corruption and hers were bound in your abandonment of each other in this place."

"You promised me I would join my father in Prawia," he replied. Kostroma snatched his hand, but he took Marzanna's with the other. "Now I can."

"No!" Kostroma shrieked, dragging him from the goddess. "The ritual ended our divide. You can't go with her!"

But her twin just shook his head at her. "I did not know of the ritual until Marzanna warned me during our ride here. You wanted to rid yourself of the demon you'd become, but you never asked what I wanted." Something shifted on his face, now looking away from Marzanna. A smile, the soft kind he'd given her as a child, but it vanished the moment he rose to meet the goddess. "Marzanna can give me that."

What are you doing, Brother?

Whether he was deceiving her or Marzanna would change everything, but he could not answer her silent question. There was no time for Kostroma to rethink her plan. She would have to trust that the ritual had worked, because another woman had stepped from the darkness.

"Mother!" Kostroma called out. She didn't rise, though. Marzanna's magic had released her, but all she could do was stare at the mother she hadn't seen for centuries. The queen of the night and rivers, donning a wreath of winding vines on her head, its ends draping down her robes of many blues.

"The time has come," Kupalnitsa said. She walked toward them with no reverence for

Marzanna, each of her steps as fluid as a tranquil stream. "My children, have you completed the ritual?"

Kupalo nodded. "We have."

"Then take to the woods until I signal otherwise. That includes you, Marzanna."

"You do not command me, but you are right in this instance," Marzanna replied with the final *S* sound carrying on longer than necessary. That alone would've been enough to make Kostroma shiver if she weren't so fixated on her mother's arrival. "Come, Minna."

The szeptucha emerged from a cluster of trees nearby. Normally an imposing presence, she stumbled to her goddess and dropped to her knees. Surely she didn't always act like this around Marzanna. Minna had claimed multiple times to be her most valued szeptucha, but she looked like a foolish girl fawning over a warrior who sought her hand.

Not long after they had all found their way to the trees, the sky seemed to open. Two bright lights converged. One came from the east, the other from the west, arcing toward another flickering sphere to the north.

Kupalnitsa stared up at the lights, but Kostroma kept her gaze on her mother.

Reuniting her family meant protecting both Simargł and Kupalnitsa. If Marzanna had turned her brother against her, then that would be more difficult than she'd anticipated. Her army wasn't far, but signaling for their aid wouldn't change things now. This was a battle between the gods. Better Timo and his men stay focused on the fight to the east afterward, when Marzanna would send the Horde after Kostroma for her defiance.

The two lights soon met the third and descended, growing ever larger in the unnaturally bright night sky. Kostroma held her breath. Simargł had to be the one from the north, and part of her feared what he'd be like after centuries of imprisonment. Her father had never possessed great patience. Would he scorn Kostroma for failing to release him for so long?

As the trio of lights neared, Kostroma covered her eyes with her arm to protect herself from blindness. The Zorza sisters were the goddesses of dawn and dusk—her aunts. They had never been particularly fond of Kostroma as the daughter of midnight. Now she understood why.

Zorza Poranna exuded morning's golden light as Wieczorna shone with the dimmer, yet no less stunning, oranges and reds of the setting sun.

Their tall kokoshnik crowns signified the sun's position in each of their times. Their dresses, too, matched their brilliant colors with streaks of warmth slicing down their skirts and streaming through the air at their feet. Everything about them was the opposite of Kostroma's dark mother, but she wouldn't have had it any other way.

Even the combined lights of dawn and dusk were dwarfed by the massive bald man between them. His height was nearly twice that of the average mortal man. Defined muscles covered every part of his exposed torso, as if trying to push free of his skin and unleash his power over the world. A single rope tied his hands together, but Kostroma sensed the magic binding them with her renewed divinity. She sought Simargł's gaze. He didn't meet it, staring instead at the ground, his bushy ashen beard burrowing into his chest.

"Simargł," Kupalnitsa said in a tone no softer than the one she'd used with Kostroma. "Why do you look away from your wife?"

The three gods' feet struck land at the edge of the river, just the smallest of trickles skirting the back of their ankles. Kostroma knew she needed to act. Fear no longer held her, but there was something else—an understanding that what she was about to do would change the Three Realms forever.

"He remains ashamed of defying Swaróg," Poranna said proudly. "Why would he not be?"

Kupalnitsa stepped closer, and Kostroma followed the motion. Keeping to the shadows, she crept to the tree line and let *žityje* pulse at her fingertips. She *was* a goddess of fertility. The lords of the Three Realms had taken it from her, and she would have her vengeance.

Wieczorna gave a dull grin. "Maybe it is time for his imprisonment to end, and for his suffering to end with it. Simargł's death would free us of this horrid ritual."

Now.

With a nod to Kupalo out of the corner of her eye, Kostroma burst from the woods. All she needed to do was blast Simargł's bindings with her *žityje* as Kupalo did the same. Twin gods uniting. Her mother had hinted at the power in that unity, and it had to be enough to free him— if Kupalo followed along.

Footsteps advanced to her left. They were behind, so she couldn't tell whether they were Kupalo's or someone else's, but it didn't matter.

If he abandoned her again, they were doomed anyway.

She drew all the *žityje* she could. Then she plunged it into the river, calling forth two spires of water that shot into her father's bound wrists. The magic in them waned but held—only half beaten.

Her breaths slowed as she waited for the second strike. *Come on, Brother!* The Zorza sisters raised their arms and summoned shields of light, but Kupalnitsa extended her arms, keeping their shields apart and leaving an opening for Kupalo. It would not hold long.

It seemed an eternity before *žityje* crackled at Kostroma's side. Pure and bright, it rushed from Kupalo's swirling hands in a golden spiral. God of summer, joy, and peace. Master of magic. He glowed with power as the spell left his grasp.

Kostroma smiled, letting the hope fill her chest. This didn't mean he'd sided with her over Marzanna, but once Simargł was free, he could make things right. He could make his son—

A mighty gust ripped across the river and met Kupalo's ball of *žityje* midair. Kostroma's blood boiled watching it deflect overhead. Part of her had hoped Strzybóg wouldn't come, but as the elderly wind god appeared above with clouds dancing at the end of his gray robes, she itched for a fight. He'd torn that wreath from her head. Now, she'd tear his head from his shoulders.

The space around the river turned to a cacophony of explosions as Marzanna joined the fray with Minna. Light, darkness, ice, water, and wind all collided, sending stray streaks of *žityje* slicing everywhere. No step was safe, not even for a god.

Strzybóg flew above it all, blowing his horn in a horrible melody that hammered Kostroma's mind. She charged after him, launching waves and spiraling towers from the river, but she didn't get far. The winds picked her up and launched her into the nearest tree. A *crack* ran up her spine. Broken, her back collapsed, forcing her to slump to the ground as Strzybóg shook his head down at her.

"Not all of us wanted this, young one," he said, his aged voice amplified by the winds. He seemed a frail old man compared to Simargł, but his force was no weaker than the legends. "I am not Perun. I admitted my errors of the past, and I would mend them if you choose a different path."

Žityje stitched Kostroma's back together slowly, faster than when the demon had been in control. She glared up at Strzybóg through the process and ignored the rest of the battle. She'd done her part, so freeing Simargł was up to Kupalo now. All she could do now was keep Strzybóg distracted and make him hurt.

Unfortunately, it was she who suffered.

"There's no other way to fix this!" she grunted.

Strzybóg sighed. "Your path is a river, and like a river, the most direct path is often the wrong one."

A scream interrupted any reply. Zorza Wieczorna's light vanished as she slumped forward, held aloft by a spike of ice sticking from her heart to the ground. Another wound bled at her neck, and Marzanna cackled before her with crimson coating her sickle blade. Kostroma's stomach turned at the goddess's death.

It's only temporary. All gods all come back, even if we shouldn't.

Temporary or not, the world seemed to shift in that moment. The slightest shudder beyond the material, as if the *žityje* in her soul recognized a force being snuffed out of the Three Realms. Poranna cried out for her sister but held up her shield. It was the only thing standing between Kupalo and Simargł now. With only one Zorza left against three gods, the end seemed inevitable. Some sorrow came with that.

Kostroma shook herself out of the daze. They could not upset the order of the gods without changing Rod's balance, so she forced herself to focus on her own opponent as her back healed enough for her to fight.

Thinking her defeated, Strzybóg turned away with a disappointed huff. He spun his arms, preparing a whirlwind to aid Poranna, but taking his eyes off Kostroma was a mistake. She staggered to her feet. One chance to hit while he was distracted. Once chance at revenge. Water seeped from the half-frozen ground as she slowly stepped toward him. It twisted around and around until it formed a vortex around her legs that mimicked Strzybóg's use of the winds.

When he attacked, so did she.

The whirlwind ripped toward Kostroma's allies, but she trusted them to handle themselves. She was already aloft, carried by the rising tide. Strzybóg didn't notice her advance until the waters had already reached him. Kostroma willed the rest to rise toward the god as one wave. Too late to defend himself, Strzybóg fell amid the water's great weight.

Kostroma tumbled after him as the vortex left her legs. Momentum carried her enough, though, and as she commanded the wave to turn back to its twisting maelstrom, she lashed out with her claws.

I am a goddess, yes, but you never stop being a demon.

Her prey's flesh peeled before her like so many she'd faced before. Gods bled like mortals all the same, and crimson poured into the vortex as Strzybóg helplessly fought against its pull. Kostroma grinned, impaling her claws into his sternum to hold her aloft as she glared into Strzybóg's light blue eyes. Fear filled them.

"I didn't want this, old man!" she screamed in his face, mocking his words. "I wanted to live, to be free! But my life was a joke to you."

"I…" Blood dripped from his gaping mouth. "I am truly sorry."

"I am not."

She plunged her second set of claws into his chest. Wounds deep enough to pierce the lungs and heart, but not enough to kill. When she drew them back, she followed the stab by digging her teeth into his neck, savoring the blood that ran down her throat. He was a god with plentiful *žityje* for her to devour. Even death wouldn't take all of it from a major god, as he would keep a receiver to recover with. Until then, she would drain him of every drop she could.

"Kostka!" a voice called from ahead, pulling Kostroma from her *žityje*-induced stupor.

A vile feeling struck as she released Strzybóg's limp body and dropped with him to the ground below. It was cold, empty. Reality paled in comparison to the rush she'd felt draining her godly victim. She'd tried alcohol, sex, and smoking herbs the mortals used to get high, but this was pure power. Taking another being's life force was a gift from her soul's corruption. This was more. Strzybóg was a god, and a god that had ruined her life at that. She thanked the darkness that regaining her godly form hadn't taken this from her.

Enough, she told herself. *Focus on your family.*

She rose, swallowing both her pride and discomfort, and looked toward the river as a blast reverberated across the field of flowers. Kupalo's hands were extended toward their father. Golden light illuminated his binds before they shattered.

Simargł was free. He rose with massive eagle wings sprouting from his shoulders. Flames burned in his mouth, and Kostroma let out a relieved laugh as Kupalo smiled back at her.

Then they froze.

Ice formed around each member of her family in less than a heartbeat as Marzanna held her curled fingers before her. Black vapors froze within each block, making it look as if the gods were burning.

"You have your revenge, as promised," Marzanna hissed at Kostroma. "Now Simargł is mine."

Kostroma tried to reply, but her body refused. A chill crept from her feet up her legs and torso until a layer of ice covered her. There was no breaking free. No matter how much *žityje* she forced into the ice, it neither melted nor cracked, and Marzanna had already turned to Simargł. Minna stood behind, staring at Kostroma with daggers hanging from her fingers.

I lost, Kostroma realized. *My father, my queendom, all of it.*

Minna would become the Lady of Rolika, the Three Realms would fall with Simargł's flames under Marzanna's command, and Kostroma would never reunite her family. It was a failure. And it was all her fault. She'd tried to best Marzanna at her own game. Instead, she was nothing.

15

Vida

HOW IS SHE THIS POWERFUL?

Vida trembled behind the goddess she'd once called Lady Marzanna. In minutes, the winter queen had killed a Zorza and allowed Kupalo to slay the second. Then she'd frozen Kostroma's entire family as if it were nothing. Four gods, all entombed in ice.

It had seemed that Strzybóg's appearance would change the course of the battle. Part of Vida wished it had. Maybe then Marzanna would've been dead, and this entire nightmare could've been over. A foolish desire. Kostroma had torn him apart in her blood rage. Revenge was a powerful force, and Vida envied her ability to take it. Despite Marzanna standing just strides before Vida now, what could a szeptucha do to stop a goddess? To make her suffer for the years of torture she'd inflicted upon her 'pet'?

Kostroma looked to Vida with her expression fixed in a mix of horror and rage. Why not at Marzanna? It was her who'd trapped Kostroma's family. All Vida had done was try to stay alive amid the fury of the gods, and she'd succeeded at that. Three gods lay dead, yet the mortal—if Vida could even consider herself that anymore—lived on for once.

But that haunting gaze…

Vida studied the goddess whose throne she would take if she stayed true to Marzanna's commands. Kostroma wasn't the terrifying demon she'd expected when she first stepped foot in Rolika. Yes, she surrendered to her miawka desires often, but there was something else in her soul, a passion worthy of a goddess. She manipulated people through understanding what they wanted. Maybe that direction could change now that she'd regained her divinity. Maybe she could be the queen Solga needed.

Why look to me? Why not trust your brother or father?

The answer was obvious as Marzanna approached Simargł. When even the god of fire had fallen to her ice, there was no one who could stop Marzanna but one who wielded her own power. Radojka had shown Vida her goddess's darkness. Only she could shatter its frozen core.

Ice daggers stung against her fingers. They were far from Thunderstone, and she doubted they could truly damage the goddess of their force. She had no other weapons. No magic that could shatter Marzanna's traps or break her defenses. It had to be a surprise, quick and direct. She had worshipped Marzanna less than an hour before, but now she had to literally stab her in the back.

Marzanna's chants hung across the windless riverside as she pressed her hand upon Simargł's forehead. The unnatural stillness made Vida conscious of every breath she took, each bit of dirt shifting beneath her feet as she advanced. She had to stay calm. Marzanna couldn't expect something was wrong, but panic rose in Vida's chest. Another death would surely be her last. Minna had never feared death with the knowledge her goddess would bring her back. Vida, though, remembered everything now, and she knew the cost of each new life Marzanna had given her. An endless prison.

A Frostmark began to form over Simargł's brow. Gods weren't supposed to be marked, but what Vida had seen changed everything she knew about the world. Marzanna commanded Czarnobóg, so why couldn't she do the same to Simargł?

I have to stop this.

The last steps to reach Marzanna felt like miles. Vida held her breath with each, forcing herself to keep her eyes open and not risk missing with the stab. She didn't, and the dagger pushed into the goddess's spine with surprising ease. The second dagger followed. Except it never found the mark.

Marzanna spun, grabbing hold of Vida's throat and lifting her with little effort. Black seeped from her claws and spread across the szeptucha's skin. Death itself devoured her now, and there would be no return.

"So you found your memory," Marzanna hissed. "A shame. You were moments away from becoming a queen, but now you'll be nothing more than food for the vultures."

Vida sputtered a reply, barely able to speak with her throat constricted. "I'd… die… serve… you…"

The pressure released, and Vida dropped to the ground. She heaved for each breath. The darkness kept spreading across her skin, pain slicing her thoughts along with it. But she'd felt this before. Marzanna had used the torture to break her once. Not again. She wouldn't lose her mind ever again.

Marzanna clicked her tongue. "You could have been so much more. Unfortunately, I have wasted enough time on you."

A creaking came from ahead, and Vida struggled to raise her gaze. The sound had been unmistakable—ice breaking. More came from every side. Marzanna noticed too, and Vida held a small fragment of hope as the goddess rushed back to Simargł, chanting again.

She's desperate.

Kostroma and Kupalo broke free simultaneously. *Žityje* glowed in their hands as Kupalnitsa followed, her own power shrouding the area in darkness. The bright souls in the night sky vanished along with the moon, but the moonlight still illuminated the space within the veil she'd created. Dim, haunting, the circle of light grew smaller as the twins launched their strikes at Marzanna. The wound had healed on her back. Ice reached for her enemies once again, but she was weakened, distracted.

Water rushed over Marzanna, grabbing her into a vortex that tore her from Simargł as Kupalo's spells hit. She hissed at the blows, but even that barely seemed to wound her. Three against one wasn't enough.

Then came the heat. Like the rising sun, it vanquished the chill amid a storm of fire. Simargł rose with his wings pushing enough air to create great gales that battered Vida. She struggled to protect her face against the wind and flames, but behind her raised arms, she grinned through the agony. The legends had told her enough about Simargł. Seeing him fly before Marzanna with flames shooting from his throat made them all too real, and she was just glad he was on her side.

"Leave this place!" Simargł's booming voice echoed. "I have resisted Swaróg and Perun's control, and I defy yours too, daughter of thunder. We could have allied against our enemies. Instead, you have chosen to burn with the rest!"

A jet of fire shot from his mouth at Marzanna. She crossed her arms, summoning a shield of ice that scattered the flames around her. The force knocked her back, and as she dug in her heels, the shield thinned. Melting, it sent water trickling down to her feet, where it rose again with Kostroma's power.

"Remember my promise," Marzanna shouted to Kupalo. "Join me now, and I will give you all of Prawia you've ever desired. You can be king among the heavens!"

The upiór bared his fanged teeth, his muscled arms extended at his side like a warrior before his final charge. White, pure *žityje* flashed within his grasp. "You promise only lies."

He threw his hands together in a deafening *boom*. The sound shook the ground itself, and the air vibrated like a wave until it crashed into Marzanna's shield. At first, the ice seemed to hold. The goddess laughed.

Until her shield split.

Marzanna screamed as the flames rushed through the gap and swallowed her whole. Vida rolled to the side to avoid the blast herself, ending up in the waters, fighting just to stay conscious. She felt the darkness spreading further across her body. It would kill her soon, and with Marzanna's corruption still haunting her veins, she would be doomed for Oblivion.

She forced herself to look when the flames stopped, hoping to see the charred remains of Marzanna. This nightmare would be over. She took some heart in knowing she'd helped that end.

But what she found instead was an empty hole in the Kupala-da-Miawkas. Ash and embers filled the space Marzanna had stood moments before. The air reeked of smoke and the blood of the fallen gods. It would've been a terrifying sight in any other context, but Vida laughed. Maniacal, ridiculous, it hurt her aching body. She didn't care. Somehow, they'd won, and she was free from Marzanna's control, even if for only a moment.

Kostroma rushed to her father as he returned to his human form and took her in his embrace. She looked tiny compared to him, but Vida knew her power. Maybe she couldn't set all of Jawia ablaze, but Vida hardly wished to stand in her way ever again.

"Come, Kupalo," Simargł said, reaching his hand out to his son. "I was trapped for an eternity fighting to avenge you, and I will not have you running from me any longer."

Kupalo relented and staggered to him. Simargł took both his children in his arms, giving a loud, blustering laugh and smiled at Kupalnitsa. "Centuries I have waited for this moment, my dear. We are together, and we can finally make Perun pay. Swaróg's children have ruled the Three Realms for too long."

The shadowed form of Kupalnitsa approached the three with her palms pressed together before her. She appeared pleased yet sorrowful. "We will never be safe. My sisters should not have had to die for your freedom, but Perun sends them to fight his battles while he feasts in Prawia!" Her voice cracked. "I just want us to be safe…"

"We will be when they are dead," Simargł said.

Kostroma nodded. "Along with their worshippers."

Vida tried to claw herself free from the river, spitting out water and blood. "They don't all deserve death."

"Oh, Minna!" Kostroma rushed to her and pulled her to the shore. Her touch was more tender than Vida had expected, but it was welcomed. "You saved us. Why?"

Resting her head back on Kostroma's arm, Vida took a long breath. Her vision blurred. *Not long now.*

"My true name is Vida," she panted, unable to give any more. "Marzanna claimed me after no god wanted me as their szeptucha. She took my memories during my time in her realm at Nawia's edge. She tortured me, drove me insane until I loved to kill for her. I don't know why she thought me special, but each time I died, she brought me back in a worse state. Only my sister could help me remember."

"Sister? I didn't see anyone?"

"Radojka, my twin. She fled, as Weles only allowed her to come her and save me, nothing more." She coughed. "If Weles sent her, maybe he's not as bad as you think."

Kupalo scoffed, crossing his arms and approaching them. "I spent years trapped in Nawia with Weles. The only mercy he gave me was allowing me to Ascend under his supervision. He would've used my power to his will if the rest of the gods hadn't decided to ruin our lives instead."

"I don't know enough about the gods," Vida admitted. "But Kostroma, I know you care about your people. You seek to know them, and that doesn't have to be making them your victims. Kupalo, you've been denied your birthright, but you can take that without creating a war between the gods. They rejected me too. Maybe there's another way."

"Kostka, you should keep this one," Kupalnitsa said. "She is wiser than she appears."

Kostroma gawked at her mother. "You just called me Kostka again."

"Reuniting our family deserves recognition. You have proven me wrong, but if you do not cease staring at me like an infant, then I will alter my opinion again." Kupalnitsa nodded to Vida, who could barely even keep her eyes open now. "Heal the girl and make her your szeptucha. We will need allies who know our enemies well."

"Please..." Vida croaked, taking Kostroma's hand. She had died many times, but she did not wish for Oblivion's eternal end. Serving The Lady was surely betting than facing that darkness. Kostroma was far from perfect, but so was she. Together, maybe they could figure out this strange world before a war between the gods destroyed it.

Kostroma muttered in the old tongue as she placed a cold hand against Vida's cheek and another over her Frostmarked eye. Szeptuchy traditionally had their mark on their neck, but she'd been no normal channeler. What came ahead would be no more normal. Despite that, Vida felt hope instead of fear. This choice was hers. For the first time in years, her life was hers to live—or end.

"Do you swear to serve me until the end of your days?" Kostroma asked. "Will you spread my name, make sacrifices at my altars, and give your life for mine if I ask it?"

The darkness crept across Vida's vision. It was still night, but the moonlight faded along with the sky's souls. All she saw now was the woman who would become her goddess. The true goddess. The true Lady of Rolika.

"I will," she breathed. "My lady."

Kostroma grinned, her hand glowing over the Frostmark. Burning pain followed, but Vida was too numbed to it to tell the difference. She was dying. What was more pain on top of her agony? It finished quickly, though, and the darkness receded from her vision along with the pain. All of it.

"Rise, Vida," Kostroma commanded with her hands lightly taking Vida's. "Rise, and help me show the gods how wrong they were about us both."

With their ritual complete, Kupalnitsa nodded and turned to Kupalo. "My son, did Rod not grant you the force of peace along with your magic?"

He winced and averted his gaze. "He did, but what if peace is not an option?"

"It isn't one," Simargł grunted. He gave Vida a distrusting glare, his eyes like coals just waiting for tinder to erupt. "But we will give Perun a chance. He will soil himself at the sight of me. At the least, I will take pleasure in that."

Kupalnitsa intertwined her fingers with his, laying her head upon his arm, as his shoulder was far above her. "There is to be a wedding in Prawia in less than a moon. Weles has found his lost child, born of the wild goddess, and intends to wed her to Jaryło to mend the divide between him and Perun."

"We need them divided to have any chance at intimidation," Kostroma replied. She still held Vida's hand tight, and Vida squeezed back just as hard. Something more than awe kept the szeptucha there. It made her heart flutter.

Kupalo looked to his mother. "Does the girl wish for this wedding?"

Kostroma grinned knowingly. "She does not. Otylia takes after her mother greatly, so it may not take much to ensure the lords of the Three Realms are too distracted among themselves to worry about us."

"Then it's decided," Simargł said sharply. "We go to Prawia."

"What about this realm, about Rolika?" Vida asked carefully, immediately wishing she'd bit her tongue. "We killed three gods. What will become of their forces?"

Kupalnitsa raised a hand before her. "Do you feel the eight winds? They are Strzybóg's grandchildren, but his force no longer feeds them. The air will be all but still for some time. As for my sisters…" She examined the dead Zorza sisters. "I anticipate father Dadźbóg will be disappointed in my actions. However, *he* will be trapped in Nawia as long as Poranna's morning gate remains shut. Jawia will see darkness until her return."

The night goddess's smile at that sent a shiver down Vida's spine. Freeing Simargł had been the plan, but she realized then that every god had other goals. Control of the Three Realms was a game for them. Even now, Vida was just a pawn.

Kostroma crouched, still holding Vida's hand, and picked a Kupalo-da-Miawka flower that had survived the battle. Its indigo and yellow flowers remained brilliantly colored despite the dim moon. Whether it was the magic that came with the eve of the summer solstice or something else, Vida didn't know. She doubted even Kostroma knew. That didn't matter. They had won this battle, and going forward, she would proudly bear the indigo flower as her mark. For Kostroma. And more importantly for herself.

"We are reunited," Kostroma said with a tear slipping down her cheek and the flower held toward her twin. "Bound by the past, we'll destroy the manipulators together. The Three Realms will shudder beneath Father's flames and our combined strength. The gods will fall, and in their place we shall rise."

The Lady released the flower, watching it flutter to the earth before turning to her szeptucha. "Come, Vida. Let us build a queendom worthy of protecting against the Horde."

END OF THE LADY OF ROLIKA

A Word From The Author

Beyond allowing me to show areas of the Three Realms that I can't in the main Frostmarked books, these novellas have also helped me practice new areas of my writing. The Lady of Rolika allowed me to venture into more gray main characters, and I loved being able to mold Kostroma, Kupalo, and Minna's stories around both their flaws and their redeeming qualities. Each of them has to grow. Even still, they are far from perfect. I find that compelling, and I can't wait to show you more of them in the next book in The Frostmarked Chronicles, The Deathless Sons.

If you have enjoyed reading this story, please take the time to post an honest review on whatever retailer you purchased this book from. Every review helps new readers discover the series.

To receive your free copy of The Rider in the Night—the prequel novella to The Frostmarked Chronicles—and exclusive first looks at upcoming books, join my newsletter at www.Brendan-Noble.com.

-   Brendan

About the Author

Brendan Noble is a Polish and German-American author currently writing fantasy inspired by Slavic mythology: The Frostmarked Chronicles. Through these books and his "Slavic Saturday" post series on YouTube and his website, he hopes to bring the often-forgotten stories of eastern Europe into new light.

Outside of writing, Brendan is a data analyst, soccer referee, and the president of Rockford FC (Rockford's semi-pro soccer club). His top interests include German, Polish, and American soccer/football, Formula 1, analyzing political elections across the world, playing extremely nerdy strategy video games, exploring with his wife, and reading.